When There's No-One There

Karen Element

A catalogue record for this book is available from the National Library of Australia

Disclaimer

This is a work of fiction. Names, characters, places, incidents and events, other than those clearly in the public domain, are either the product of the author's imagination or used fictitiously. Any resemblance to actual persons, living or dead, is entirely coincidental.

To all the souls, lost and found.

Chapter 1

I should have asked her if she needed anything, Marian thought, as she rounded the bend, nearly knocking Mrs Gardiner's garbage bins over. Marian loved every minute of her time before university began. High school was behind her now, with a few weeks of freedom in front of her before study began in earnest. She loved to drive – it gave her a feeling of exhilaration, as though she could fly.

I really should slow down a bit though, she thought, looking at how close she'd come to wiping the bins out. She pulled up in the driveway, yanked the handbrake on and turned off the engine. She looked over the side fence at the house next door.

Marian couldn't see her neighbour sitting in her usual place on her patio. Mrs Gardiner had her grandmother's old rocking chair positioned to catch the late afternoon sun, the sea breeze and the salty air. However, this afternoon, the chair was empty and still. Even when it was raining, Margot Gardiner would still take up her position, moving her chair under the shelter of the little awning near the front door, and watch the comings and goings in their street.

I'd better go and see if she's okay. She got out of the car, grabbed her shopping bags and locked the door. She stopped in front of the rusty old gate and glanced up at the rocking chair again. She couldn't remember her neighbour ever not sitting there, rocking back and forth humming a little tune to herself.

Margot Gardiner had sung on the stage in her time. On the wall in her hallway, there were photos of her dressed in her glamour and gripping a microphone. Her voice had not grown old 'along with the rest of her' she would say, breaking into song … but it was all silent on the patio today.

Marian's heart felt as empty as the chair – she hated its still-ness. It looked lost and alone, just like she felt, and tears stung her eyes as she stared at it. *What's wrong with me?*

She pushed hard against Mrs Gardiner's gate, anticipating its rusty resistance, but it opened as easily as if it was brand new. She stared at the gate and frowned, then glanced up again at the patio … and there she was – Mrs Gardiner – sitting on the patio in one of the chairs from the backyard. Marian's mind knew the patio had been empty a minute ago, but relief washed over her just the same as she wiped the tears from her eyes.

'I'll be over in a minute,' Marian called out, turning and closing the gate.

Mrs Gardiner waved an old, shaky hand at her and dis-solved back into the shadow. As she raised her hand to return the wave, Marian noticed that the awning above the patio needed painting, along with a lot of other things around the old house. She felt a familiar anger as she thought of the family who didn't bother with this sweet old lady – the family who did nothing to help her.

'Mrs Gardiner wasn't in her rocking chair today,' Marian said to her mother as she came through the back door into the kitchen, spilling her shopping bags onto the table. It was cold outside but the oven had been on and its warmth still hung in the air. Marian took off her jacket and sat down at the kitchen table; her thoughts focused on the house next door. 'She must have dragged one of those chairs from the back yard to sit on,' Marian continued. 'Beats me how she got it up those stairs and on to the patio. I wonder why she did it in the first place. She can hardly climb those stairs unaided now. She always holds onto the handrail tightly because she's afraid she'll topple over … Mum are you listening to me?'

Marian stared at her mother's back as she stood at the kitchen bench fussing with the cake she'd just pulled from the oven. Marian noticed an almost indiscernible shaking of her mother's shoulders and an alarm bell went off in her head.

'Are you trying to be funny, Marian?' Sonia said, dropping the knife from her trembling fingers as she spun around to glare at her daughter. The knife made a loud clang on the bench top, startling Marian and causing the shopping bags to slide off the table. Marian tried to stop the plastic landslide but they slipped through her fingers, piling themselves on the floor beside her chair.

'What's wrong, Mum?' Marian said, noticing her mother's flushed, tear-streaked face. *Mum never cries,* she thought, watching her mother wipe unsteady hands on the tea towel she kept slung over her shoulder.

'That dear old lady passed away last night so how can you possibly have just seen her?' Sonia snapped. Then she clapped a hand to her mouth. 'Oh, I'm sorry, sweetheart. I shouldn't be cross with you at a time like this.'

'At a time like what?' Marian spoke slowly as she watched her mother closely. *She's not making any sense.* That alarm bell rang louder.

'They said she died peacefully in her sleep.' Sonia reached for the box of tissues on top of the fridge and dabbed at her eyes.

'What are you talking about? Who died?'

'I told you – Mrs Gardiner.'

'But … she's sitting outside on her patio.'

'I know it's a terrible shock. You two were very close.'

'We *are* very close. I don't understand what this is all about.'

Sonia sat down next to Marian and explained what had happened. She'd been out by the letter box that morning after watching Marian tear off in the car, when the meals-on-wheels people had arrived next door. They'd started helping when Margot had stopped caring about herself – when she'd wanted to follow her husband into death a few years ago.

She had watched them knock on the door and when there was no answer, go around to the back of the house. Sonia told Marian how she had felt a knot begin to twist inside her when she saw them return and knock on the front door again. Then she realised they must have a key because they opened the front door. There was still no sign of Margot.

Sonia took her daughter's hand in hers. 'A few minutes later, I heard an ambulance siren approaching. Most of the neighbours rushed outside to see what was happening. Then I saw the ambulance trolley exit Mrs Gardiner's front door carrying a black body bag. I remember noticing how the sun glinted off the shiny black vinyl of the bag as it was loaded into the back of the ambulance. Then it sped off, without its siren on, before all the neighbours gathered outside her house to say their silent goodbyes. It was so sad. I can't bear the thought of poor Margot dying all alone like that.' Sonia's tears began to flow freely again.

Marian looked at her mother in disbelief, anger boiling up inside her. 'I've never heard anything more ridiculous.' Marian struggled to keep her temper under control. 'She's sitting on her patio under the awning. I saw her when I came home.' Marian snatched her hand away from her mother's and folded her arms across her chest.

'I know this is sudden,' Sonia said, 'but she wasn't a young woman.'

'Stop it, Mum! She's right outside!' Marian jumped up so fast she knocked the kitchen chair over. She ran out through the back door, her heart hammering in her chest, desperate to find out what was going on. Fear and certainty jostled in her mind as she raced down the side of the house. She looked across to the patio next door, her eyes locking on the familiar old rocking chair. Mrs Gardiner was sitting right there, exactly where she should be. Marian smiled at her and waved her own shaky hand.

* * *

Sonia bit her lip, trying to imagine what was going on in Marian's head. *She must be in shock*, she thought. She knew that denial was the first stage in the grieving process; she remembered that from when she had lost both her parents in a car accident before Marian was born. She'd needed counselling to help her deal with it all back then and she wondered if Marian would need some now. She stumbled out the back door after Marian. *What's the matter with her?* she thought, as she tried to catch up. Her own heart was racing at the thought of her daughter's pain. Sonia stopped dead in her tracks when she found Marian leaning up against the little side fence between the two houses. Her daughter was standing perfectly still, except for her right hand.

What's she doing? Sonia stared at Marian's hand moving slowly through the air. She swivelled her head to see if there was anyone around – anyone who Marian could possibly be waving at – but the street was deserted and eerily quiet.

Sonia followed Marian's line of sight to the old rocking chair, still and empty on the patio next door. She saw a hint of a smile begin to play on Marian's lips as her hand continued to wave, then freeze in mid-air when Marian noticed her mother standing closely behind her.

'Sweetie, there's no-one there.' Sonia's mind reeled as she thought of the possible reasons for Marian's bizarre behaviour. *Dear God, I hope she hasn't started taking drugs,* she thought, knowing that wasn't even remotely possible. Marian was about to commence university to become a doctor; her health was everything to her.

* * *

Marian whipped her head back around – Mrs Gardiner *was* there, rocking in her chair. She watched as the old lady pushed herself up into a standing position and returned Marian's wave. Mrs Gardiner stood up very straight with no evidence of the slight stoop she usually had. A rosy glow had replaced her normally pale complexion. *She's never looked better,* Marian thought, as she watched her neighbour in fascination.

She turned back to her mother. 'Yes there is. Mrs Gardiner's right there – look!' Marian pointed to the patio, never taking her eyes off her mother's face.

Sonia shook her head, her eyes moving from Marian's to the empty patio, where she took a second to double-check. 'No Marian, no she's not.'

'I'll prove it to you,' Marian said. She jumped over the side fence before Sonia could do anything to stop her. She needed a moment to herself to try and calm down. Her mother was making no sense and Marian was afraid of what that could mean.

Marian hesitated a little as she walked up Mrs Gardiner's front steps. 'I think there's something wrong with Mum or her sense of humour has suddenly become warped,' Marian called out, as she reached the top. She needed to talk to Mrs Gardiner about her mother's strange behaviour, but the rocking chair had become empty and still. *What? Where's she gone? She can't move* ***that*** *fast.* Marian searched the small patio with its old concrete pots filled with their pink geraniums. She tried the front door but it was locked. Marian gazed back at the old rocking chair again. *What the Hell's going on here?* She wondered if there was a hidden camera somewhere and if this would be on TV one day. She almost laughed at that thought.

Marian felt a warm sensation brush against her legs and she jumped. Snyder, Mrs Gardiner's black cat, had started winding himself around her legs. 'Aw, you must be hungry.' Marian bent down to pat the cat. 'Let's go around the back and see what's going on.'

Mrs Gardiner was nowhere to be seen in the small yard but the missing chair from the outdoor setting was back in its place. Marian drew in a sharp breath and ran back to the front of the house. *There she is,* she thought, the rocking chair occupied once more.

'What are you playing at? You really had me worried for a minute,' Marian said, racing back up the patio steps. But by the time she reached the rocking chair, Mrs Gardiner had somehow vanished again. Marian watched as the empty chair moved back and forth in a solo rhythm. She felt her heartbeat slow and the panic leave her body. Comforting warmth covered her like a blanket as she sat down in the chair. It rocked her like a baby in a cradle. She closed her eyes and smiled.

* * *

Sonia had watched Marian's strange behaviour from her vantage point. Now she stood frozen to the spot in shock and disbelief. *She's acting as if Margot's still there – as if she can really see her.* She watched Marian sit down. The rocking stopped abruptly, and Marian leapt up, staring in front of her, all the colour drained from her face. She flew down the stairs, jumped back over the side fence and took off into the house again.

Sonia gave chase but as she ran inside, she heard the door to Marian's room slam upstairs. She thought of her husband who worked thousands of kilometres away. *Damn you Craig for not being here when I need you;* a thought she'd had countless times during their almost twenty years of marriage.

A few minutes later, Sonia hovered outside Marian's bedroom door. She could hear Marian's voice saying, 'She's not dead. I saw her, I really did.'

Sonia took a deep breath to control the mounting fear that threatened to envelop her. She knocked and entered the room to find Marian muttering loudly and pacing furiously up and down on the balcony off her bedroom. She looked so unsure of herself – nothing like the assured, confident young woman she'd grown to be.

'You've had a shock. Here, come and sit down.' Sonia sat in one of the deck chairs before patting the other with her hand. Marian stopped her pacing and leant over the balcony railing. She stood very still, looking up at the sky, full of the colours of sunset.

'It's so pretty,' Marian said, sighing deeply.

Sonia wanted to get Marian away from that balcony railing. 'Come downstairs and I'll make some tea, then we can talk about it. I'll see you downstairs in a few minutes.'

* * *

But Marian didn't want to talk about it with her mother. A distant memory kept rattling around in her head, trying to piece itself together. She had a feeling of déjà vu. She'd been in this situation before – where no-one believed her and dismissed her words with indulgent smiles.

I saw her, I really did – words from another time – words she'd repeated over and over in the past. She concentrated hard – trying to sweep the cobwebs away – fervently trying to recall the memory that eluded her. She pictured her seven-year-old self, a serious look on her little face, as indulgent smiles broadened around her. Ten years ago, this'd happened before.

Chapter 2

'Marian hasn't been herself since Margot died,' Sonia said. She was sitting at her kitchen table having tea with Kath, her neighbour on her other side. 'I can't get her to open up about how she feels – she just keeps telling me that she's fine.'

Sonia had been stirring her tea for the last ten minutes. Even though she and Kath didn't have a close relationship, Sonia was desperate to talk to someone. Craig's request to fly home early had been denied, so Sonia was left to prop Marian up as best she could.

Kath had been living next door to the Whites since Marian was born. She had very old-fashioned ideas about a lot of things and minding her own business was at the top of her list.

'Would you like some more tea?' Sonia got up to put the kettle on again.

'Yes, that would be lovely.' Kath passed her cup and saucer. 'I love having tea with you, Sonia; you do it properly, just like my mother did.' Kath admired the beautiful bone china cup in her hand and thought about Marian. She'd watched her playing through their common fence when she was a little girl. She'd been hard to ignore with her laughing and squealing, but it was the quiet conversations she held with herself that Kath had found disturbing.

'It can't be easy, just the two of you, with Craig away so much of the time,' Kath said.

'Yes, I feel as though I'm both mother and father for three weeks out of four. Marian was a bit of a handful when she was little, always laughing and playing in the back yard – loud and busy in her own little world. She probably disturbed you more than once.'

'There were times when she really scared me.' Kath leaned in towards Sonia as if she was sharing a secret. 'I didn't want to mention it at the time and I don't know why I'm telling you now.'

'Scared you? I don't understand; she was only a little girl. How could you be afraid of her?'

'I understand little children and their imaginations …'

'What do you mean?'

'I could hear her when she was playing in the back yard, and sometimes, I could swear she wasn't playing by herself.'

'Yes, she had an imaginary friend – a little girl. I think she conjured her up because she was an only child. Sometimes I would join in with the game – even her father did when he was home.'

Kath shook her head, remembering the way Marian had acted. She remembered seeing her through the fence palings, throwing a ball across the yard and squealing with delight when it came flying back to her.

'It wasn't you or Craig out there with her, Sonia.'

'Well, she grew out of it by the time she was seven.' Sonia got up to rinse her teacup, signalling the end of the conversation.

Kath felt it was time to change the subject. She hadn't really wanted to talk about Marian anyway. 'It was nice to see Margot's grandchildren at the funeral – pity they hadn't visited her more often while she was alive.'

'Yes, she was such a lovely lady – she deserved so much better than that. She was always making excuses for them – they were too busy with work – they lived too far away, but the truth was, they just couldn't be bothered going out of their way for her.'

'Marian was more like a granddaughter to her than that lot,' Kath said, then made her excuses to leave. She wished she hadn't said anything about Marian. She'd managed to keep her feelings and thoughts to herself all this time, but there was something about the girl that unnerved her.

* * *

After Kath went home, Sonia sat at the kitchen table wondering about her daughter. She hoped it was only time she needed. She'd been so quiet since the funeral – nothing like her usual bubbly self. The little Jeep sat silent and idle in the driveway, while Marian lay on her bed all day, staring into space. Sonia didn't know what to do. She thought they could talk about anything, but not this – not death.

The back door opened suddenly and Marian appeared in the doorway, shivering and wet from the rain. Sonia was startled out of her reverie by her unexpected arrival. 'I didn't know you'd gone out,' Sonia said, jumping up from her chair. Rivulets of water snaked their way down Marian's soaking clothes, which were plastered to her body like a second skin.

Sonia grabbed a towel. 'Here, wrap this around yourself.' She offered Marian the towel, but Marian stood there like a statue, the shivering coursing through her body her only movement. Sonia draped the towel around Marian's shoulders, rubbing her arms to generate some warmth.

'Where have you been? I didn't hear the car.' The blank expression in Marian's eyes terrified Sonia. 'Did you hear me, Marian?' But the stony silence continued as Marian shrugged the towel off her shoulders and took a step towards the kitchen window. It offered a sweeping view of the back yard. The rain was getting heavier, thrashing itself against the house. The warmth in the kitchen had caused the windows to fog up, making visibility impossible.

'Marian, you need to get out of those wet clothes.' But Marian continued to stare through the rain into the yard.

Sonia picked the towel up off the floor and gently placed it back around Marian's shoulders. She could feel them shaking through the towel. She held her tight, rubbing her arms again. 'I'm so worried about you. This is the first time in your life someone you know and care about has died – it's a big thing for you, I know.' *She can't go on like this. I'm going to have to get her some help,* Sonia thought.

'Can you see her, Mum?' Marian's voice was barely a whisper as she pointed to the kitchen window. Marian's eyes were as glazed as the window as she continued to point through the deluge.

'Who? Who can you see? What's out there?' Sonia shook her head. 'Come on, we need to get you out of these wet clothes before you catch your death.' She winced at her choice of words but Marian hardly seemed to notice. She let Sonia lead her from the kitchen, up the stairs to a warm shower and some dry clothes.

Sonia left Marian under the warm water and came back downstairs. She dried the wet floor with an old towel she kept for rainy days and put the kettle on again to make some more tea.

She went to the cupboard to fetch a cup for Marian, but her shaky hands lost their grip on the smooth china and it smashed on the floor.

Sonia bent to pick up the pieces, scolding herself for being so clumsy. She held the shards of china in her hand, saddened by the loss of one of her mother's prized possessions. Emotion overwhelmed her that had nothing to do with the cup as the tears began to fall. She went over to the window and wiped a small section of it with the sleeve of her jumper.

The rain had eased somewhat and as Sonia peered into the yard through the drizzle, she could see nothing out of place. *Everything seems alright … apart from Marian.*

Chapter 3

'Oh, look at this one, Therese,' Sonia said.

Sonia's sister nodded and glanced at the photo Sonia was pointing to. They were flicking through some old photo albums, looking for any pictures they may have taken of Margot. Sonia had come across one of Marian in Therese's back yard.

Oh God, not again. She'll never let me live that day down, Therese thought, hoping she wasn't going to hear all about what a fabulous mother Sonia was – how *she* would never have lost Marian. She'd been looking after Marian at her place that day at the house where the sisters had grown up and which Therese had never left.

'That was a long time ago now. I'll never forget that day,' Therese said. *You'll never let me forget.*

'Yes, we never could account for that missing hour.'

'I couldn't find her anywhere; I was out of my mind. I looked everywhere for her – everywhere.'

* * *

The sun had been shining that day, so Therese had sent little Marian out to play in the treehouse. Therese's father had built it for his daughters and now Marian was the lady of the house. They all loved the sturdy little construction nestled high in one of the many trees in the large back yard.

Therese could hear girly giggling through her open study window as she rushed to meet her editor's deadline. She was so focused on the article she was writing, she didn't realise when the laughter had stopped. She ceased her furious typing and went out into the yard to investigate, but there was no sign of Marian.

'Marian, where are you? This isn't funny you know,' Therese yelled, as she climbed up to see if Marian was hiding in the treehouse. Puffing and panting, Therese looked over the little window sill, but the treehouse was empty. She climbed over it and searched the yard from the high vantage point but there was still no sign of her.

Therese climbed back down to solid ground and tore around the back yard, the front and all through the house searching every nook and cranny, but Marian had vanished. Therese had grabbed her phone to call the police when she heard the crying.

'Where were you?' Therese gasped, discovering Marian standing on the ground underneath the treehouse. Marian was inconsolable. Therese gathered her up in her arms. 'Are you hurt?' Therese let her go long enough to check for broken bones and bleeding, before she carried the distraught little girl inside.

Thank God, Therese thought, dizzy with relief when she could find nothing wrong. She tried to talk to Marian to find out where she'd been for almost an hour but she couldn't get any sense out of her. Marian had just clung to her and cried. She was still distressed when Sonia came to pick her up a few hours later.

* * *

'I guess we'll never know what really happened, Sonia, but I wish you'd just let it go.'

Sonia slammed the photo album shut and turned her back on her sister as she leant on the kitchen bench. It was early evening and Therese was staying for dinner. There was a pile of fresh vegetables on the sink. Sonia grabbed an onion and began to take her frustrations out on it.

'Need any help?' Therese said. When her sister ignored her she thought, *Oh, great – the silent treatment.* She wandered into the hall and up the stairs. Therese stood outside Marian's door listening for signs of life. It was silent on the other side of the door and there was no answer when Therese tapped on it lightly. She tried the knob and it opened easily.

'Hi Therese,' Marian said, turning her head towards the opening door. 'I was just thinking about you and here you are.'

'It's nice to be loved.' Therese sat down on the edge of the bed and looked closely at her niece. 'Didn't you hear me knocking?'

'No, I guess I didn't.' Observing Marian's red, swollen eyes and seeing her lying there like that caused Therese's eyes to prick with tears as well.

'What's going on, honey? Your mother's very worried about you.'

Marian shrugged her shoulders and remained silent. She was dying to talk about everything – she needed to, but she didn't know where to begin. Marian opened her mouth to speak, but nothing came out. She'd rehearsed what she'd say a hundred times in her head. It had sounded almost reasonable there – nearly plausible, but saying it out loud was a different story.

She couldn't talk to Therese about any of this ... or her mother. She couldn't tell anyone because she didn't know ... she couldn't explain ... what was happening to her. Marian knew Mrs Gardiner was dead. She'd been to the funeral. She'd seen the coffin being lowered into the freshly dug hole in the ground.

There was a "For Sale" sign in the front yard next door and Mrs Gardiner's family had visited one last time to take what was left of her life. Marian had gone over that day while they were sifting through her few belongings looking for the good stuff, but there wasn't much left. Margot had given them all she had while she was alive in a lonely effort to get closer to them. Marian cried when she saw the sad heap, ready for the bin. She picked up one of the pictures that had hung in the hallway – all glitz and glamour, and it was pride of place in her room now. She'd been staring at it where it hung opposite her bed, when Therese had knocked on the door.

Marian could still see Mrs Gardiner … and not only in the picture. Sometimes it was only a glimpse out of the corner of her eye, but other times she was standing right there – right in front of her – smiling and nodding her head, before she faded away.

Now she said to her aunt, 'I'm okay – really, I'm fine.'

'You know I'm here if you need me – anytime, for anything. Your mother and I were just talking about the day I couldn't find you when you were seven. I'll never understand how you hid from me for almost an hour.'

Marian thought back to that day. She'd been playing with Raven in the treehouse, giggling with her in their make-believe world. Without warning, Raven had jumped out of the tree-house window. Marian screamed and rushed to the window, but Raven hadn't fallen. She was just outside the window floating in the air. Marian now recalled their conversation in vivid detail.

'I think you're old enough to know now,' Raven said, mis-chief flickering in her shining eyes.

'What do you mean?' Marian stared at Raven, transfixed on the emptiness beneath her feet.

'You need to know how special you are.'

'I don't like this game, Raven. Come back in.' Marian stepped aside to make room for her but Raven shook her head and grabbed Marian by the hands.

'Come on, I want to show you something.' Raven pulled Marian out through the window – out into the air with her. 'See, you can do it too.'

Marian lunged for the window sill, clawing at the air around her, but she couldn't reach it. She closed her eyes, waiting to fall, but instead she floated gently like a balloon full of helium. She opened her eyes and looked towards the ground. All the fear left her as she stared back at Raven in wonder. Marian moved her legs, just as if she had the earth beneath her. She walked vertically down towards the ground with Raven by her side.

'Can we do that again?' Marian said, gazing up towards the treehouse. Raven shook her head and began to back away.

'I can't play with you anymore,' Raven said.

'Why not? Have I done something wrong?' Marian's lower lip began to tremble. Raven was her best friend. Marian didn't want anything to change.

'No, you haven't done anything wrong. It's just that you're growing up and you don't need me anymore.' Then she kissed Marian on the cheek and skipped away laughing. Marian stared after her. She couldn't understand what Raven was talking about.

'Raven, Raven – wait for me, don't go.' Marian ran as fast as she could, trying to catch her, but Raven was too quick. She was gone. Marian couldn't find her anywhere. She slumped against the bottom of the tree, crying as though her heart would break.

Marian looked up at where the two of them had been playing. She spied Raven up there through the branches. She was free-floating, up and away from her. Marian watched her go – watched her rise higher and higher, a speck disappearing from her life.

* * *

Therese watched as Marian remembered that day. She could see the emotions play and change on Marian's face. She saw her look at the picture of Mrs Gardiner and noticed how her eyes filled with fresh tears. *You're not okay,* Therese thought, wishing she'd open up to her but she took the hint and didn't push. She sat with her and held her hand. She couldn't reach her but she wanted Marian to know she was there.

Chapter 4

Craig was coming home. His plane was due in a few hours and Sonia was busy making herself beautiful. This homecoming day was particularly significant. This time Sonia was sure she could make Craig finally see that money wasn't the most important thing in the world. He'd worked away for too long. It was too late now to make the second baby Sonia wanted. But she didn't care about that now. The baby they already had was in trouble. She was sure he would see for himself that he needed to come home now.

Sonia always bought a new dress for Craig's homecomings and Craig always noticed. He noticed everything about her and he would know something was very wrong as soon as he laid eyes on her today. She checked her makeup in the bathroom mirror and went to fetch Marian.

* * *

'I'm so sorry that I couldn't come home for the funeral – you know how this job can be,' Craig said as he jumped into the car. He leaned over to kiss Sonia but she turned her head and he had to settle for her cheek.

'You look beautiful.' Craig admired the new dress and everything else about his wife.

He loved her. She was his queen. She deserved the best that money could buy. 'And how's my other favourite girl?' Craig checked the back seat but his heart sank when he saw it was empty. He turned to Sonia, disappointment showing in his eyes. And he had been so looking forward to this homecoming.

'Where is she? Is she outside somewhere?' He went to open his door but Sonia put a firm hand on his arm.

'She said she didn't feel like coming. I told you on the phone; she's not right.'

'She's as bad as that?' Marian had never missed a homecoming day before. He was beginning to realise how serious things were. He didn't say any more – he knew what was coming.

'If you were here, you'd know.'

'Not now, Sonia.' He didn't want to get into the same old argument. He just wanted to get home to Marian.

They drove the rest of the way in silence. It was not the day either of them was expecting. Homecoming day was their only red-letter day in the month, but this one had just lost its colour.

Marian was sitting on the front steps of the house in the sun, waiting for them to come home.

'Dad, I'm sorry I didn't come to the airport.' She jumped up and threw herself into her father's outstretched arms. She put her head on his shoulder and started to cry.

Craig held her close, waiting for the storm to pass, as Marian clung to him and emptied out her tears.

It was too much for Sonia to see the emotion pour out of her daughter. She spilled some tears of her own as she caught Craig's eye and saw her own concern reflected there.

* * *

'She's sleeping now,' Craig said. He'd gone upstairs to say good night to Marian and to see if she was alright. It had been very quiet around the dinner table that evening. Usually, none of them could get a word in edgeways with all of them talking at once. There was always happiness and an urgency buzzing in the air on their first night back together – glad to be a party of three again. They would sit there until all hours glued back together with the love they had for each other, but it had been very different on *this* first night.

Marian had wandered off early to the isolation of her room. *She's not herself,* Craig thought, as he'd watched her leave. He'd now seen for himself how withdrawn and quiet she'd become.

'What did she say?' Sonia said.

The troubled look on his face answered her question. 'I tried to get her to talk about things – about how she feels, but she didn't say much.' Craig sat down at the table, shaking his head. 'I tried to talk to her about loss – about what it's like when we lose someone, but she didn't seem as though she was really listening.'

* * *

In her room, Marian *was* listening. She was trying to understand what the little boy standing at the end of her bed was saying. He sounded very far away but he was so close, Marian could almost reach out and touch him. *Is he speaking a different language?* she thought, as she struggled to make sense of the words.

'You'll get used to it,' another voice said that Marian *could* understand. 'You just need some time.'

'Wh-what?' Where was that voice coming from? It wasn't coming from the boy. Never taking her eyes off him, Marian crept out to her balcony. There was a girl out there leaning on the railing. She turned her head and smiled.

'I didn't want to leave you, Marian, but they gave me no choice,' she said, her radiant smile dimming a little. 'Aren't you pleased to see me?' The smile now disappeared almost completely as the girl stood wringing her hands.

Marian couldn't move. She couldn't think. Her eyes could see the girl but her mind refused to accept her standing there. 'It's me,' the girl said. 'Don't you recognise me?'

Marian stared at this apparition coming to life from somewhere deep in her memory.

She looks older – she's all grown up! 'Raven!' Marian rushed to the railing, forgetting about the boy, forgetting about everything else. 'It's so good to see you.'

Then Marian remembered the last time she'd seen her and what they'd done up there in the trees. *This isn't real. I must be going crazy.* She took some deep breaths and leant against the railing next to Raven, feeling the freshness of the sea breeze on her face. She closed her eyes for a moment to try and steady herself as she listened to the waves crashing and wondered if she was hallucinating. After a moment, Marian opened her eyes and looked straight into Raven's piercing green ones.

'So, you've come back – why?' She forgot about questioning her sanity. It didn't seem so important as she gazed at her oldest friend.

'To finish what we started – come on.' Raven began to rise, effortlessly moving up through the air. Marian watched her, remembering the last time she'd seen her float away.

'Wait for me!' Marian felt the nothingness under her as her body left the safety of solid ground. Like a balloon tethered to a small child's hand, she hovered a few metres above the balcony, marvelling at the detailed delusion she was experiencing. She waited to fall, but she felt solidity surrounding her, keeping her safe.

* * *

Sonia's hand froze mid-knock outside Marian's bedroom. She'd come up to check on Marian and heard her talking to herself. It sent her back to another time, when her little girl had played by herself with her imaginary friend – a time of childhood innocence – childish fun, but Marian wasn't a little girl any longer. Sonia had pressed her ear up against the door. The talking seemed to fade then stopped abruptly. She knocked softly but there was no answer.

She can't have fallen asleep that quickly, Sonia thought, so she opened the door quietly. She found Marian standing out on her balcony looking skyward, with a big, bright smile on her face.

Is she sleepwalking? Sonia wondered, watching her daughter's odd behaviour. She remembered reading somewhere that it was dangerous to wake someone if they were in that state. Sonia hesitated, not sure whether to enter the room or not. She started to back slowly away from the doorway, being careful not to make any noise. *Craig needs to see this.*

* * *

'Mum, wait,' Marian called out as her mother started to close the bedroom door. 'I'm OK.' Her mother's worried face appeared again. Marian's bright smile had scarcely diminished.

'Don't worry, Mum, I really am okay.' *Now that Raven's back,* Marian thought.

'What were you doing out there?'

'I was looking for Heaven.'

Sonia smiled and reached out, brushing a stray hair off Marian's face. 'You used to say that when you were little.'

I used to say a lot of things when I was little, Marian thought.

Chapter 5

'You need to stay Craig … you know you should,' Sonia said, her lips pressed into a thin line.

They were on their way back to the airport. Craig knew Sonia was making a final effort to convince him not to go.

'You know I have to get back to work. It won't last forever.'

'You need to be here for Marian.'

'She seems fine now.' Craig glanced at his daughter in the rear-vision mirror. She seemed engrossed in whatever music she was listening to, the headphones jammed in her ears. 'I'm sure she's nearly over it.'

'No, Craig, she's not over anything. I wish you'd listen to me. It can't be a good thing that she's started talking to herself again; she hasn't done that since she was seven.'

Sonia moved her head a little, so she could see Marian in the rear-vision mirror, then she looked at her husband and nodded her head towards the back seat. Craig turned the angle of the mirror slightly so he could see Marian. He saw the animation on her face and he saw her try to hide it when he caught her eye.

'You alright back there?' Craig said. He could see Marian's lips moving as though she was speaking to someone, not singing along to her music.

'Marian, what's going on?' *She's not listening to me,* he thought. Craig's knuckles turned white on the steering wheel. 'Okay, okay – I'll see what I can do,' he said to Sonia. He could see why his wife was so worried now – he realised he needed to be home with his girls.

When they arrived at the airport, Craig got out and Sonia slid behind the steering wheel.

'I'll try, I promise,' were his parting words to his wife. He leaned in the window and kissed her gently on the lips – he really didn't want to go. He opened the back door so Marian could slide out and move into the front seat.

'Look after your mother while I'm gone.' He hugged her tight, said a silent prayer, and then he was gone.

* * *

'Do you want me to drive?' Marian asked when she noticed the single tear coursing its way down her mother's cheek.

Sonia shook her head. She was unsettled enough without the added terror of being in the car with Marian behind the wheel.

'He'll be back before you know it,' Marian said, watching the tear drip onto her mother's hand. As she reached for it with both of hers she stole a fleeting glance into the back seat.

'For God's sake, Marian, what are you looking at?' Sonia snatched her hand away and turned around.

Raven shook her head at Marian. 'Now's not the right time, Marian.'

But Marian was finished with all the secrecy. 'Raven, Mum. I'm looking at Raven.'

'What did you say?' Sonia's eyes frantically searched beyond the back seat, through the back window of the car.

I should have kept my mouth shut, Marian thought.

'Yes, you should have. The timing's not right,' Raven whispered as she melted into the back seat.

'You can read my mind?' Marian said.

'What are you talking about?' Sonia stared at her daughter, a frown creasing her brow as she waited for an answer.

'Mum, could we talk about this later? I'm really tired.' Marian closed her eyes and remembered back to when she was four or five – when Raven had first come to play.

* * *

Marian and her mother had been at the beach near their house. A little girl had sat next to Marian on the warm sand.

'What's your name?' the little girl said.

Marian looked up from the serious work of building a sandcastle. 'Marian – what's yours?'

'Raven … can I help?'

Marian nodded and they set to work. They built a sandcastle like the beach had never seen. There were soaring spires and intricate tunnels that emptied and filled with water as the waves rolled in and out. They had laughed and giggled as the masterpiece came together.

'Would you like to go and get some ice cream?' Sonia asked, coming over to inspect the work of art. 'Marian, that's a truly wonderful sandcastle – I've never seen anything like it. Where did you learn to do that?'

'Raven showed me.'

'What a beautiful name,' Sonia said. 'Who's Raven? Where is she, Marian?'

'What do you mean? She's sitting right there.' Marian pointed to the empty space beside her on the sand. 'You're playing a funny game, Mummy. Come on Raven, let's go.'

* * *

Now, Marian opened her eyes and twisted around to stare at the back seat again. *Where is she?* Marian thought, willing Raven to return.

Sonia was still staring at her, her face flushed with exasperation. 'Marian, for the last time, what're you talking about?'

'Nothing, it's nothing.' Marian turned around and put her seatbelt on.

'Come on then, we need to go home.' Sonia moved carefully out into the traffic, using the side mirrors to check for on-coming cars, resisting the urge to look in the rear-vision mirror. She had a strangle hold on the steering wheel to stop her hands from shaking as she tried to concentrate on the road.

Chapter 6

During the drive home, Marian took her phone out of her bag. She hadn't felt like talking to anyone since the funeral so it had been on silent. She noticed all the missed calls and texts.

The number she called was answered almost immediately. 'There you are – thank God, I've been so worried,' Bronte said. 'I haven't seen you since the funeral but I wanted to give you a little time to get over everything but it's been over a week.'

'I'm okay. I'm sorry, Bron, I should have called.' Marian knew Bronte would hear the strain in her voice. Bronte had been around for a long time – long enough to know when her best friend was in trouble.

'Do you want to talk about it?' Bronte asked.

Marian cast a sideways look at Sonia. *Mum's had enough for one day,* Marian thought, noticing Sonia's white knuckles gripping the steering wheel.

'I'm in the car with Mum. We're on our way back from the airport.'

'Oh, that's right – your dad went back to work today. Do you want me to come over later?'

'I'll call you when I get home.' Marian switched the phone setting to silent again and slipped it back into her bag. She closed her eyes and rested her head back against the seat.

Raven's not real. She's just a real figment of my imagination, she told herself.

* * *

'So how is she? Is she okay?' Therese said. She had come over to see her sister and niece after they got home from the airport. She knew how much Sonia hated the day Craig went back to work. She'd watched them for years – her sister … and the man *she* had seen first. There had been a thing between Therese and Craig, nothing serious, at least not on his part, but the torch still burned brightly for him in Therese's lonely heart.

The two sisters had taken up their usual positions at the kitchen table with the teapot between them.

'She's talking to herself again,' Sonia said. 'She's saying that Raven's back.'

'What are you talking about?' Therese remembered the Raven game and how insistent little Marian had been that she was real.

'She told me. She *sees* her.'

'What?' Therese nearly dropped her cup.

'She wouldn't believe me when I first told her that Margot was dead. She insisted she was still alive. She even waved to the empty rocking chair.'

'I don't understand. What do you mean?'

'She hasn't really said anything since the funeral so I guess she's accepted Margot's death by now, but this Raven thing …'

The two women let what that meant hang between them for a moment.

'It must be stress related,' Therese said. *What else could it be?* She wondered why Marian had brought her childhood friend back.

'I think there might be something wrong with her,' Sonia reached out a shaky hand. Therese grabbed it, feeling the tremor course through her own body.

'It's just her way of coping. She'll be fine – you'll see. What did Craig say?'

'Oh, don't get me started about *him*. He was no help whatsoever.' Sonia almost threw her teacup down. It clanged loudly in its saucer and nearly broke.

Therese resisted the urge to roll her eyes. She'd heard this all before. 'But, what does he think?' Therese couldn't believe he wasn't concerned; he would move Heaven and Earth for his family. That was one reason she loved him so much.

'It's the same old story. He had to go back to work.'

Therese moved to the sink to fill the kettle again.

'I'll make you some chamomile tea. That always settles your nerves.' *And a double-dose of a sedative for me, if I must listen to your complaining,* Therese thought.

Sonia nodded, smiling through her tears and dabbing at her eyes with a tissue.

'I think I'll go and talk to her,' Therese said, placing the fragrant tea in front of her sister. 'Do you mind?'

'No, of course not. Maybe you can help me get to the bottom of this.'

Therese could hear Marian's animated voice as she got closer to her bedroom door.

She must be on the phone, she thought, creeping closer. Therese pressed her ear to the door to hear what Marian was saying. She couldn't understand the words but she could sense the serious undertone in her voice.

* * *

'Therese is on the other side of the door. Can you see her?'

Marian almost burst out laughing at the serious look on Raven's face. 'How can I see her? The door's shut.'

'Yes, but if you concentrate you can see through it. You can *see* her.'

'I haven't got time for this. Therese's out there.'

'Invite her in – yes, it'll be just like old times.'

Marian shook her head and reached for the doorknob. 'Therese, what are you doing out here?'

Marian pulled the door open so fast, Therese nearly fell into the room. 'I came over to see how you were. I didn't want to interrupt your phone call.'

Oh God, she heard us, Marian thought, casting a sideways look at Raven. 'I'm okay. Come in and talk to me.' Marian stepped aside to let her pass, but Therese didn't make a move.

'Actually, could we go for a walk or something instead?'

'Okay, let's go down to the beach then.' Marian turned back to look over her shoulder for Raven but she was gone.

'We're just going for a walk,' Therese said, poking her head into the kitchen on their way to the front door. Sonia was still sitting at the kitchen table. 'Would you like to come with us?'

'No, you two go ahead. I'll get some lunch ready while you're gone.'

* * *

'I haven't been down here for a while,' Marian said, watching the waves crash on the shore. 'I love the glorious feeling of the sand between my toes.'

'I thought this was your favourite place in the whole world.' Therese watched her expression closely. Marian didn't answer; she just stared at the ocean. *God, what do I say to her?* This was going to be harder than she thought.

'Your mother's very worried about you.' Therese waited but the silent staring continued. 'Marian, did you hear me?'

'I've had a lot on my mind. Raven's back.'

'I don't understand. Raven isn't real, honey – you know that.'

'Don't think I don't know how this sounds, but I can see her as clearly as I can see you.' Marian smiled at Raven as she materialised on her right.

Therese watched the change in her niece – the way she gave the empty space next to her her full attention.

'And I know you know she's here.' Marian now focused her full attention on Therese.

Oh, my God, she's serious, Therese thought. 'No, I don't know anything of the sort.'

'Then why couldn't you enter my room? You felt something, I know you did.'

Therese's mind spun in shock. She remembered the weird feeling she'd had when she looked inside Marian's room. Something had seemed different but she didn't know what. Suddenly, her legs couldn't seem to hold her up. Her knees buckled and she sank down into the soft, warm sand. 'I just need to sit down for a minute.'

'Are you alright?'

'I'm okay but I can't understand what's going on with you.'

Chapter 7

'I need you to tell me the truth, Raven, and I want to know right now,' Marian said. 'This is affecting more people than just me.' After the scene at the beach with Therese, Marian was desperate to get to the bottom of what was really going on. 'I need to know if my mind's intact or not. I hate feeling like this.'

'Well, I'm the last person you should be asking, don't you think?' Raven said, as she tried to hide a smile. 'You believe in me – that's half the battle.'

'But I don't understand what's happening to me. Maybe I need to talk to a shrink or something.'

Marian was determined to get to the real reasons now. She wanted to know – she needed to understand. She stormed out to the balcony and flung herself into a chair. She closed her eyes, trying to let the sound of the waves soothe her jangled nerves.

'You give me no choice, Marian. But I warn you, it's a lot to take in and you need to keep an open mind.' Raven's voice broke through Marian's efforts to stay calm as she sat down in the chair next to her.

'And having you around isn't a lot to take in? Just get on with it – tell me.'

'I'll start with a question. What do you think happens to us when we die?'

'I don't know, I haven't really thought about it all that much. But I guess *you're* dead, aren't you?' Marian's anger evaporated, as she pondered the question. Raven stood up and leant on the railing. She turned around and smiled.

'In a way, but it's more like existing in a different space. The body withers but the soul grows stronger.'

'So the guise you appear to me in is your own?'

'Yes, this is what my body looked like before it failed, albeit a few years older. I appear to you at the same age as you are and I've changed the way I dress to be more like you.'

'What happened to you, Raven?'

'I was very sick. They didn't have much in the way of medicine back when I was alive.'

'My God, how old are you?'

'Old enough, but let's not get off the subject here. When you were little, you didn't question anything. Your mother and aunt played along with you, so you had no reason to think there was anything wrong. I had to leave you before you thought there was.'

'I don't understand. You left me. You broke my heart because I was growing up?'

'Not intentionally. We were just trying to spare you any heartache until you were old enough to handle it. We've found that up until the age of about seven, children believe what they see and what they're told, without question. All the fanciful things belong to them – Santa Claus, the Tooth Fairy, monsters under the bed, imaginary friends, you know – things like that.'

'So you left before I stopped believing in you, before I started to question things, and then you came back when you thought I was ready to understand, is that it?'

'Something like that. You're destined for great things – things that haven't even been invented yet.'

One thing at a time, Marian thought. Her head was reeling with questions and her imagination threatened to run riot.

'You keep saying "we". What do you mean by that?'

'Well, you don't think I'm the only one, do you?' Raven jumped over the railing and floated in the air.

Marian gazed at this impossibility. *This is so surreal – like a real delusion.* She closed her eyes and saw her body floating free. She felt that nothingness around her again. That solid nothing, that held her tight.

'What do I do with this?' Marian opened her eyes, feeling the weightlessness as she hovered just above the tiles on the balcony.

'Let me show you.' Raven beckoned Marian to join her. Marian rose up and over the railing. She bobbed in the air next to Raven. They began to move up through the air, past the trees, higher and higher. Marian felt the lightness in her body, and a warmth surrounded her like the protection of an old friend. She looked down, seeing nothing but specks of colour where she'd left her life. She absently thought of her mother and wondered what she'd think if she came to her room and found her gone.

'Don't worry about your mother – time has no meaning up here.'

'Would you stop reading my mind?' Marian said, as she let the air currents propel her gently up through the clouds.

* * *

Downstairs, Therese was sitting with Sonia at her kitchen table, the place where they sorted out all the problems of the world. She remembered long stints sitting here with the tears and the teapot after her husband was taken from her in a car accident. Manny had been no Craig, but he'd been a good husband to her. Therese was here again, trying to make sense of what Marian had said while they were down at the beach, and she was trying to understand what she had felt while she was down there with her. Therese had sensed something as soon as Marian had surprised her at her bedroom door, and the feeling persisted.

Since arriving back at Sonia's she hadn't said a word. She had sat down at the table, let her head rest in her hands and stared into space. She was a million miles away until at last she stared directly at Sonia.

'She's convinced that Raven's real.'

'What!' Sonia looked hard at Therese. 'And you believe her?'

'She said Raven came back after Margot died.' Therese ignored her sister's question. She left out the part about the feeling she'd had. She needed to think about that on her own for a while.

'Well, she must be hallucinating or having a breakdown or something.' Their tea had grown cold. Sonia got up to make a fresh pot. 'Do you remember Mina? Did you ever think *she* was real?'

Therese thought back to her own childhood and her own special friend. 'She felt real enough to me at the time.'

Chapter 8

It was like the second chance Marian had been waiting for since that day so long ago, when she'd watched Raven disappear from her life. Marian could feel the softness of the clouds on her face as they swam through them and beyond. The blue of the sky began to change to sunset pink, then to a deep magenta.

Raven pointed to a speck in the distance above them. As they got closer, Marian could see a vast expanse of water the same colour as the sky. Its edge was lush with greenery, lit with iridescent light that bathed everything in a warm glow.

Marian thought she could see people by the lake. She was suddenly afraid. There were definitely figures sitting by the water's edge watching her approach.

As Marian and Raven brought their feet to rest on solid ground, the people waved and smiled. They formed a little group, coming to greet them with open arms. They surrounded the two girls, pressing in on them. Marian began to feel a little claustrophobic as the crowd continued to push. Suddenly, the throng parted, making way for a solitary lady to come forward.

She's so lovely, Marian thought, mesmerised by the way she majestically glided towards her, her tight silver curls framing her ageless, porcelain face.

'Marian, I'm so glad to meet you at last. Please don't be concerned, my dear. Raven has brought you here because it's time you were told the truth. Allow me to introduce myself properly. My name's Imogen and this is The Magenta Sky.' She extended both arms to reveal her glorious domain.

Marian absorbed the beauty surrounding her – a vibrant, living thing that cloaked her in a peace she'd never known. All the cares of the past few weeks evaporated as she returned the beaming smiles that were shining her way.

The people came in closer; old, young, men, women and children. They didn't clamour. They didn't crowd. They just stood quietly in silent worship.

'Is this Heaven?' Marian said. A ripple of laughter made its way around the group as they all looked at Imogen.

'No, my dear, but we're very close.' Another small ripple erupted before the people dispersed, leaving Marian, Raven, and Imogen alone by the lake.

'Thank you for bringing Marian safely to us, Raven.'

'You told me the time was right,' Raven said.

Marian detected a hint of sullenness on Raven's face. But Imogen didn't seem to notice as she smiled at Raven warmly.

'I thought this may make the transition smoother for you – a familiar face.' Imogen pointed to somewhere over Marian's left shoulder. Marian turned around and looked straight into the eyes of Mrs Gardiner. The world fell away as Marian fainted. 'Take her back, Raven,' Imogen said. 'She's not ready for the rest of us yet.'

* * *

'Are you alright?' Raven said, leaning over Marian, concern ripping through her voice.

'Where am I? What happened?' Marian said, trying to sit up but the weakness coursing through her body won the battle. She realised she was lying on her own bed.

'Your first trip to The Magenta Sky seemed to be too much for you but you'll be fine after you rest for a while.'

'The Magenta Sky exists?' Marian tried to sit up again but she fell back against the pillows.

'Yes – look, you stay where you are and I'll try to explain it all to you.'

Marian watched Raven pace through the air and thought she looked like she was full of helium. She could feel hysterical laughter threaten to erupt. *I really am going out of my mind.* Marian tried to concentrate on what Raven was saying.

'I thought going up there would help you understand but I should have explained the situation a little better first.'

'Keep your voice down, I don't want Mum to hear us. She's always skulking around outside the door.'

'You've been blessed with special abilities, Marian. You can visit the dead before you die and you can see the dead while you still live. There are many of those among the living who are able to catch a glimpse of us, but to see what you see, go where you can go is more than a miracle.'

'Is Therese able to see?' Marian held her breath, waiting for the answer.

'She has selective powers of sight. She can see if they want her to see. But she has an acute sense of knowing – she can sense when one of us is around.'

'I knew it. I knew that she knew,' Marian said, almost beside herself with excitement.

'Don't worry about Therese. We'll get to her later. You need to focus on yourself right now.'

'Okay, one thing at a time. As you were saying?'

'I was sent to watch over you when your soul decided it was ready to be born.'

'You mean, like a guardian angel or something?'

Raven nodded her head enthusiastically. 'Exactly – we all have guardians, angels and spirits that are assigned to us, or volunteer for the job, like Margot Gardiner has with you.'

'Mrs Gardiner? She's with me?' Marian thought about the dear old thing and she could feel the love wrap itself around her. *She hasn't left me. No wonder I see her everywhere.*

'Yes, Margot's on your team with Imogen and me. Often there is more than one soul – people who love you and don't want to let go, and others who are sent to teach and guide.'

'So there really are two worlds – this one and the one up there.' Marian cast her eyes up to the sky.

Raven drifted out to the balcony. Marian tried to sit up again and realised her strength had returned. She followed Raven outside. She found her leaning precariously over the railing.

'If I knew you couldn't fly, I'd tell you to be careful.' The smile faded from Marian's lips as she caught the dark, foreboding look on Raven's face.

'We mustn't forget the world down there.'

'You mean it's really there – down there?' Marian's hand shook a little as she pointed to the ground.

'Yes, it exists. You can't have one without the other. There are two sides to every story, you know. Two sides to everything. All existence is entwined, one way or another.' Raven smiled again but a shadow persisted that sent a shiver up and down Marian's spine. 'But don't worry about that now, either.'

'The Magenta Sky is so beautiful; its opposite must be a dark, evil place,' Marian said, a second shiver coursing through her body. 'I want to understand. Tell me what you know.'

'Well, there's right here – where we are now and there's up there – a place beyond our dreams. Beneath us is a realm of darkness, a place where nightmares are born.'

'Like Heaven and Hell?'

'Sort of – it's not as simple as that.'

'What do you mean? I don't want there to be any kind of Hell,' Marian said.

'Well, apart from The Magenta Sky, we have The Grey Dusk. Two places, before the end of each spectrum, where all final decisions are made. We're given the opportunity to be sure of the path we wish our destiny to take.'

'So, you can change your mind – your direction?' Marian leant over the railing and looked down at the hard, unforgiving ground. Then her gaze drifted upwards as she thought about the bright, airy place she now knew was up there. This was a lot to process. It wasn't all black and white, but it seemed organised, and it made a kind of sense to her.

'In extreme cases, a soul can make it all the way.'

'I like the idea of a second chance,' Marian said, her eyes drawn back down to the ground. 'But the thought of a hopeless place, somewhere beyond death, terrifies me.'

'Yes, they're a special breed, down there in The Blackness.'

'What do you mean? What do you know about it?'

'Only what I've heard – what others have told me.' Raven didn't want to talk about it. She leaned over the balcony and stared down at the ground with a look of longing on her face. 'As a naked soul, we can do all sorts of things we could never do while we were still alive. This is a dead kind of thing, you know?' She began to levitate and somersault in the air.

'What are you talking about, Raven? I'm not dead and I can do it … but maybe I am dead. Maybe that's what this is all about.'

'No, you aren't dead – you're unique – you're alive, but you have abilities bestowed only on those of us who *have* lived. Sure, we have mediums, psychics, people like Therese who can scratch the surface, but you … *you* have the powers of the dead.'

'But what is it that I'm meant to do?'

'That's just it – no-one anywhere knows. You'll grow into this, Marian. You'll become your own shining light. You'll glow in the dark for all of us.'

'I'll never get tired of this,' Marian said as she floated upwards again, feeling the air beneath her. 'I still don't understand what I'm supposed to do with this but I guess I'll find out eventually, one way or the other.'

'You're unique, the first of your kind; the first to ever enter The Magenta Sky before death. You have transcended the barrier between here and there without dying. Who knows what you are truly capable of?'

'Let's go up there. I want to try it again.'

Chapter 9

'Hi honey,' Therese said, as Marian opened the front door. 'You ready?'

'Ready for what?'

'We're supposed to be going out for lunch. Where's your mother? Didn't she tell you?'

'Oh, she mumbled something about needing to get out of the house for a while.'

'She must have forgotten I was coming over. How're you feeling?'

'Better – I feel better. I think I've gained a new perspective on things.'

Therese frowned. *I wonder what she means by that?*

'I'm sure Mum won't be too long – come in.'

In the living room, Therese smiled at two stunning women sitting on the lounge. She could see that one was Marian's age, but the other was older. *My age – probably the girl's mother,* Therese thought. The two strangers shared no physical resemblance; the younger woman had flaming red hair while the older one had long black tresses, but Therese could feel a connection between them. 'Oh, I'm sorry,' she said. 'I didn't know Marian had company.'

Therese glanced at Marian who seemed to be silently signalling to the other two women.

'Hello Therese,' the older woman said, getting up and extending her hand. 'It's been a while.'

'I'm sorry, do I know you?'

'We were friends a long time ago. How could you forget?'

Therese looked long and hard at the familiar stranger. She had a flashback to her childhood, when her serious sister had told her there was no Santa Claus; when she refused to play with her, calling her a baby. She remembered how lonely her childhood had been until the day she conjured a little friend to fill the void. Therese came back to the present and stared at the older woman who nodded and bowed her head. Therese followed her gaze, becoming transfixed by the tiny gap between the woman's gold sandals and the carpet. Her mind refused to accept what her heart was trying to tell it as the room began to swim before her eyes.

'Therese, Therese are you alright?' Marian bent over Therese's prostrate form. 'Raven, what've we done?'

'She'll be alright – maybe that wasn't such a good idea, Mina,' Raven said.

'I didn't expect her to see us. We should have kept ourselves hidden. I guess I got a bit carried away,' Mina said.

'I didn't think she'd see you two either,' Marian said. 'I think I'm too terrified to be excited.'

'This's a major step forward for her,' Mina said. 'All this time I've been watching, waiting for her to open her eyes again.'

'Will she remember this when she wakes up?'

'Would you like her to know?' Mina asked.

Marian wasn't sure. She didn't know what she wanted right now – apart from erasing the last few minutes. She hovered over Therese who was pale and unconscious on the floor. 'I want her to know the truth, but I don't think she's ready to re-believe.'

'I think that's the right decision,' Raven said. 'We don't want *her* questioning reality too.'

'No, we don't,' Marian said, feeling her own grip on it slip a little more. Raven sat down on the floor, gently placing her hand on Therese's head. Mina stood behind her, softly touching Raven on the shoulder. They stayed that way until their bodies faded away to nothing, taking Therese with them.

* * *

A minute later, Sonia burst through the front door. 'I forgot all about Therese and lunch,' she said.

'Did you have a nice walk?' Marian said, dragging her eyes away from the now empty space on the floor where Therese had been.

'The ocean always clears my head. Isn't Therese here yet?' Sonia glanced at the clock on the wall. 'I'll call her and see how far away she is.'

Far enough, Marian thought, grabbing her car keys and rushing out the front door.

'Where're you going? Don't you want to come out with us?'

'I'm going to see if she's still at her place.' *I need to see if she's there. I need to know she's alright.*

'Wait for me, I'll go with you.'

But Marian was already out the door. She didn't hear her mother, as she backed out of the driveway and tore up the street.

* * *

Therese lived about half an hour away but Marian made it in fifteen minutes. She banged on the front door but there was no answer so she raced around the back, nearly breaking the latch off the side gate in her haste.

'Therese, Therese, where are you?'

'What's all the fuss? What's the matter?' Therese looked up from the overgrown garden bed she was weeding.

'Aren't you supposed to be having lunch with Mum?'

'Ahh … I forgot. But why the panic?' Therese couldn't fathom Marian's behaviour or the wild look in her eyes.

'You're supposed to be with Mum. She's waiting for you.' Marian jammed her hands on her hips and glared at Therese.

'Okay, okay. Could you please calm down and tell me why you're so concerned about me being late for lunch?'

Chapter 10

'Where is she?' Sonia said, finding Therese standing at the bottom of the big tree looking up into the branches. She'd broken half the road rules in her attempt to catch up with her daughter. She'd found Marian's little Jeep with the driver's door open in Therese's driveway. The side gate was hanging on its hinges, so Sonia ran that way.

'She's up in the treehouse.' Therese pointed skywards, the worry etching lines in her face.

'She flew out of the house as if the Devil himself was after her,' Sonia told her sister.

'Yes, she was nearly out of her mind when she got here, babbling something about lunch with you.'

'I don't know what to do with her, Therese.'

* * *

Marian sat in the treehouse trying to make sense of nonsense. She didn't know what to believe anymore. 'Not now, Raven,' Marian said, as she watched Raven's floating form appear at the treehouse window. She wasn't in the mood for talking to anyone – dead or alive. 'I just need some space. Could you leave me alone for a while?' She looked over the side fence into the back yard next door. She could see Lisa, who she'd known since they were both little, standing out by the clothesline.

Marian realised she needed her friends – her real friends.

'Hey Lis.' Marian waved frantically to catch her attention. Lisa looked up towards the sound. She waved back enthusiastically when she saw Marian up in the treehouse. 'Can you come over?'

When Lisa arrived at the bottom of the big tree she found Marian's mother and aunt looking grim faced. 'Hey Therese – hello Sonia, what's up?'

'Maybe you can find out for us,' Therese said.

'Yes, Marian might talk to you,' Sonia said, nodding her head.

'Is she alright?' Lisa said, shading her eyes against the midday sun, as she craned her neck to see the treehouse. But both women just shrugged and ushered Lisa up the tree.

'Haven't seen you in a while,' Lisa said, climbing through the window. 'I was very sorry to hear about your neighbour – Therese told me.'

'Oh that … thanks. Hey Lis, remember the fun we used to have up here?'

Lisa nodded. 'Are you okay, Marian? You look terrible.'

'And trust you to tell me.' Marian attempted a smile but it died on her lips.

'What are friends for?' Lisa sat down next to Marian on the old soft drink box that had been recycled as a chair. 'So, what's the matter?'

'I'm just tired, I guess. I haven't been sleeping very well.'

'Are you worried about starting uni?'

Marian shook her head. She'd given little thought to her next move in life. Recent events had taken over everything. 'I think there's something wrong with me …' Marian's attention was caught by Raven floating silently through the treehouse window. 'I don't suppose there's any chance that you see her?'

Lisa followed Marian's gaze to the empty space in the middle of the little room. 'No, but I can see that you can. Tell me about it …'

* * *

'There's no right or wrong,' Raven said, after Lisa climbed down. They could hear her talking softly with Sonia and Therese. 'You just have to do what you think is for the best. It's all part of you becoming who you are meant to be – your most authentic self.'

'On one level, I know you and Mina were at my house earlier, but on another, I know that's impossible.'

'Why? You see me don't you? Now you need to *believe* that you can see me.'

'I saw you and Mina fade away to nothing. I saw Therese lying on the floor and I saw you take her with you.'

'I promise you, there are no lasting effects from being moved. I transported you back from The Magenta Sky and you're okay.'

'You call this okay? I'm *not* okay.' Marian's voice rose to a crescendo as she threw herself out of the treehouse and grabbed hold of the first thing she could – a minor branch that barely held her weight. It started to crack and splinter as Marian swung back and forth. 'Do you hear me, Raven?' she shouted up at the treehouse.

At the base of the tree, Therese was the first to react. She bounded up the ladder but slowed her pace as she approached Marian and steadied herself on a big branch below her.

'I don't know what's happening to me,' Marian said, as she looked down and saw Therese beneath her. 'But I can fly, you know.'

Therese watched in horror as Marian took one hand off the branch. She gauged the distance to the treehouse was closer than the safety of the ground. 'Marian, listen to me,' she said. 'Climb back up to the treehouse and we'll talk.'

'Marian, it's too high,' Sonia screamed from the ground. 'Go back!'

'Come on – up you go,' Therese said, her voice as shaky as the rest of her body.

Marian remembered what Raven had said. She saw the terror in Therese's eyes and heard the raw panic in her mother's voice. She grasped the branch with both hands and began to climb.

'She's alright. We'll be down in a minute,' Therese yelled down to her sister. She tried to steady herself as she positioned her body on the ladder between Marian and the window.

Once inside the safety of the treehouse again, Marian sat down on the soft drink box. 'So, you really don't remember coming to our place this morning?'

'I was supposed to have lunch with your mother. I was meant to be at your house today, but I guess I forgot.'

'You never forget anything.'

'Marian, can we both forget about *that* for now? We need to do something about what's been going on with you.'

Marian took a deep breath and decided to try her luck. 'I'm telling you – Raven is here – Mina's with you, and that's all there is to it.' Marian watched Therese's eyes widen and thought her aunt was finally beginning to waver.

'I know you're not lying to me, but I can't accept what you're saying as any kind of truth,' Therese said.

'Why can't you? We're both sitting in this treehouse – a place where we both know anything's possible. For God's sake, close your eyes and *see*.'

Therese forced her eyes shut but the impact of Marian's words caused her confusion to clear. Her eyes flew open again.

She'd never mentioned Mina to Marian. 'How do you know about Mina?'

'I told you – I've seen her.'

'Did Sonia tell you?' Therese needed to know how Marian knew – Sonia was the only plausible explanation.

'Could you imagine her talking about something like that?' Marian was very hopeful that Therese was starting to believe her but at Therese's next words she sighed.

'You know what? Let's get down. I don't want to talk about this anymore.'

I shouldn't have said anything, Marian thought. *She's not ready.*

* * *

'Slow down, Sonia. I can't understand a word you're saying,' Craig said.

'She nearly fell out of the tree. You have to come home right now Craig, *please.*'

'What tree? Is she alright? Is she hurt?'

'She's not hurt, but she's not alright.'

'Tell me what happened.'

'Craig – you don't understand – she could've died.'

'You haven't left her alone, have you?'

'No, she's up in the treehouse with Therese.'

Craig thought she must be exaggerating as he listened to this fantastic tale. 'I'll catch the next flight home,' he said and ended the call.

Sonia had been so intent on getting through to Craig that she hadn't noticed Marian standing right in front of her. 'You need help – *we* need help,' Sonia told her daughter.

Marian shrugged her shoulders. She walked slowly back down the side of Therese's house and out the front to her car. The door was hanging open, just as she'd left it. Marian got in and shut it. She reached into her pocket for her keys but her pocket was empty.

'This what you're looking for?'

Marian turned her head in the direction of the jangling noise. 'Give them to me,' she said, snatching the car keys out of Raven's hand. Marian struggled to find the right one, then she jammed it into the ignition, but she didn't start the car. 'I can understand why they're so worried – I'm worried,' Marian said.

'You have to stop making such a spectacle of yourself,' Raven said.

'That – from you?' Marian threw back her head and laughed.

'Think about it. Whether I'm here or not, they can't see me. All they know is that you're sitting alone in this car, talking and laughing to yourself. How do you think it looks to them?'

'So, what you're saying is, I should act as if everything's okay?'

'Yes, get the spotlight off yourself. Keep it quiet. You need time to grow into this – time to discover all the wonders waiting for you.'

Marian got out of the car and locked it carefully. Sonia, Therese and Lisa had followed her to her car and were standing nervously by the letter box, watching and wondering what she was going to do next.

'I'm sorry, Mum,' Marian said as she saw the worried looks on their faces. 'I don't know what came over me. Maybe I'm having a nervous breakdown or something.'

'Your father's coming home,' Sonia said.

'What did you say to him?' Marian demanded, imagining the phone conversation, with her mother on the brink of hysteria.

Sonia flinched at the sound of her raised voice.

'You didn't need to tell him to come home, Sonia. We've got things under control,' Therese said.

'If this is your idea of having things under control, then I'd hate to see your idea of chaos. Mind your own business, Therese. He's my husband and I'll tell him whatever I like.'

'Therese thinks a lot of your father,' Raven had moved to Marian's side and now she whispered in Marian's ear. 'Maybe a little too much.'

'Don't be ridiculous,' Marian said.

'It's ridiculous that I have to deal with all this without him,' Sonia said, glaring at her daughter.

'You're not dealing with anything. You never do. Why is it always worse for *you?*'

'What are you talking about?'

'This is about *me*, Mum. Something's happening to *me*, not you.' Marian went back to her car. Her hand shook as she tried to put the key in the lock.

'Where're you going, honey?' Therese said.

'I need to get out of here.' *So much for staying out of the spotlight,* Marian thought.

'I'll come with you,' Lisa said. She put her hand on Marian's and took the car keys from her. 'I'll drive.'

* * *

'You didn't handle that very well,' Therese said, as she watched the car drive off down the road.

'And I suppose you could have handled it better?'

'I *was* handling it, until you dragged Craig into it. I could hear you from up there – screaming and carrying on.'

'You just stay the hell out of my business, Therese.'

'Marian *is* my business. Don't you think it's funny how she raced over here, away from you when she needed help?' *That may have been a bit much,* Therese thought, as she saw Sonia's face crumble, but she wasn't in the mood for regrets right now.

'Damn it, Sonia! You need to open your eyes – you need to see what's really going on here.'

'And what would *that* be, she-who-knows-everything?'

'I don't know everything.'

'Then, what do you *think?*'

'I think it's possible – just possible that there might be something else going on here.'

'Like what? What do you mean?'

'Maybe she's telling the truth – maybe she *can* see things that we can't.'

'I thought we were going to have a meaningful discussion here, but I can see you've got your head in the clouds as usual.'

'And you've got yours buried in the sand.'

Sonia threw a scathing look at Therese and stormed off down the driveway to her car. She was so angry she dropped her keys in the gutter when she tried to open the door. She scooped them up and drove off without a backward glance.

Chapter 11

Marian stood in the bathroom doorway watching her mother. She was exactly where and how she'd left her – in front of the mirror, doing her makeup. She watched Sonia apply a perfect lip pencil line and expertly colour her cheeks to a flattering glow.

Marian had been up to The Magenta Sky, sat by the lake with Imogen, and spent time listening to the unfinished business of the souls in her care, all before Sonia had finished applying her lipstick. The slowing of time made Marian's travelling seamless – undetected. She could spend hours up there, but by the time she had floated back down, only a few real seconds had passed in the world below.

* * *

'I want to explain things to you more clearly now,' Imogen had said.

Marian sat with her feet dangling in the cool, pink water. 'I love it here,' Marian said, gazing around the rim of the lake, returning the smiles that came her way. *Tranquil and lush, with a hint of slow urgency*, was how she would describe The Magenta Sky.

'Yes, but there's work to be done.'

Marian stopped her musings and caught Imogen's shining eyes. 'Work? What kind of work?'

'A gift has been bestowed on you, Marian – indescribable and unique.'

'Everyone keeps reminding me but I still don't understand what that really means.'

'Neither do I, but we have all been watching and waiting for the energy you now possess to reveal itself – an energy searching for a worthy recipient.'

'How did this so-called energy come to exist? How do you know about it?'

'Do you know what possession is?'

'I assume you mean the spiritual kind?' *I don't know if I like where this is going,* Marian thought, shivering as she remembered horror movies she'd seen with her friends.

'Yes, but please don't be afraid. On one such occurrence, the living soul refused to be possessed. It resisted, but instead of casting the spirit out, and instead of the spirit moving on to find another victim, the two souls fused, combining to form a new energy – one never known before. This energy has lain dormant for so long that it was thought it would never re-appear. And then you came along.'

'You aren't making it any clearer.'

'I'm sorry – it's all been stuff of myth and legend, until now.'

'Now you're beginning to scare me.' Marian remembered seeing possessed beings at the movies, all moans and shrieks as they stumbled around looking for fresh victims.

'Please don't be alarmed, my dear. We believe the energy is fuelled by light – the sinister aspect of the possession destroyed by its purity. This is where your powers come from. The energy you now possess gives you wings. I can see the energy has chosen wisely.' Imogen smiled at this girl who was going to change the worlds.

'Thank you … I think.' Marian stopped her shivering and cast her eyes over the beauty that surrounded her. *This is as far away from Hell as I could get,* she thought.

'We'll explore the extent of what you can do together and you'll help the souls here while we do.'

'How can *I* help them?'

'You're able to act as a bridge between The Magenta Sky and life. You can work with these souls to tidy their affairs – to help them let go and move on to their paradise.'

Marian let her gaze rest on the people milling around the water's edge. *It'd really be something to help them,* she thought. 'I know about the other place down there – the one deep down there. Raven told me.'

'Yes, and I have no doubt that they too have been watching and waiting.' Imogen drew her eyebrows together as she looked down at the ground.

'I know there's good and bad,' Marian said, 'yin and yang, I can understand that, but how bad can bad really be?'

'There are spirits that will try to do you harm. You'll sense it, even though they may present themselves in a pretty package.'

'I don't believe anyone or anything is completely without hope.'

'And that's another reason why you've been chosen.'

Marian pulled her feet from the water and stood up. *I've got so much to think about,* she thought.

* * *

'I'm so happy your father's coming home,' Sonia said, when she caught Marian's reflection in the bathroom mirror. She checked her flawless face one more time before she left the bathroom. She went back to her room to collect her handbag from the bed before she swished her way down the stairs to the front door. 'You can drive, if you like.' Sonia flung the car keys in Marian's general direction before brushing past her in a cloud of perfume. She was revelling in her small victory of having her husband home again.

She's in a good mood, Marian thought, as she watched her mother dance down the driveway in her new dress. Marian locked the front door and followed her mother at a more sombre pace. She knew she'd have some explaining to do and she didn't have a clue what she'd say to her father. He'd never come home early from work before. *He must be worried out of his mind.*

After Sonia's frantic phone call, her mother had acted as though her problems were over. Her husband was coming home – the reasons seemed to be beside the point now.

Marian pulled up in the passenger pick-up. She could barely see her father behind the baggage trolley he was pushing. It was piled high, unsteady with a mountain of bags threatening to topple off. Marian leapt from the car and ran to help him, leaving Sonia preening herself in her mirror.

'I'm sorry, Dad,' she said, as she grabbed hold of the suitcases, trying to hold them steady.

'There's nothing to be sorry for, love. I just want you to be alright.'

Marian threw herself into her father's arms causing the bags to wobble. Then, they leapt apart, catching the pile just in time, laughing like it was the funniest thing they'd ever seen.

'Hello darling,' Sonia said, a little breathlessly, hurrying to join the family re-union.

Craig gathered his two girls together in his arms. He could feel their hearts beating against his own. As he stood there, holding all the riches in his world, he finally realised that money wasn't everything.

* * *

On the trip home, Marian tried to pay attention to what Craig and Sonia were saying while she ignored the woman sitting next to her in the back seat. She'd been there when Marian got in the car. The woman had a surprised look on her pale face, as her dull, lifeless eyes darted around, taking in her surroundings.

She's not such a pretty package, Marian thought, as she braced herself for whatever was to come.

'Am I back?' the woman said.

'From where?' Marian whispered, trying to slide inconspicuously down in the seat.

'My neck hurts.'

'What happened to you?' Marian could see the deep, red mark circling her throat.

'I wasn't finished … I need to finish.'

The car suddenly stopped and Marian realised they had pulled up in their driveway. Sonia got out and opened the front door, while Craig wrestled with the luggage in the boot.

'I don't think I can help you. You need to go,' Marian said to the strange woman. *I don't want her following us into the house,* she thought.

'Oh, but you will. You'll do exactly as I say.'

Marian felt a big lump form in her throat. She had no idea what to do.

'You heard her – Marian asked you to leave.' The voice came from a ball of white mist in the corner of the backseat. The wispy outline of a face began to take shape and Marian saw it was Mrs Gardiner coming to her rescue.

'Go away, old woman. I was here first,' the younger one said. Her dead eyes sparked with fire as she turned to face her.

'And I'll be here long after you've gone – now *go!*' Mrs Gardiner said.

A low moan escaped the woman's lips like an animal in pain. She began to thrash around, bashing her head against the backseat. The moan built to a deafening crescendo, forcing Marian to cover her ears to block out the shriek.

Mrs Gardiner seemed unaffected as she positioned herself between Marian and the noise – a steely determination settling on her face. The shrieking stopped but a sudden wind began to blow. The woman spun around with it, caught in its fury, and became part of the gust. Her features distorted, and then she disappeared along with the wind.

'Marian – what're you doing in here?' Craig said, opening the backdoor, finding her still in the backseat, flushed and breathless.

'Oh, I was just listening to my favourite song.'

Marian's earphones were in a tangled mess on the floor of the car. And they both noticed the keys still dangling in the ignition but the radio was silent.

'Ah, I just switched it off,' Marian said. She didn't want him to worry. She had seen the creases deepen in his brow. 'So, what's the plan, Dad? When're you going back to work?'

'I'm not going away to work anymore. Luckily, I've been offered a job here. But I thought I'd take a little time off first before I start – you know – to hang around with you and your mother for a while.

You mean, let Mum get her own way, Marian thought.

'The strangest thing happened, though,' her dad continued. 'I had a call from the bank, congratulating me on paying the mortgage off.'

'You mean we own the house?'

'Yes apparently we do, but I thought that was still about five years away.'

'So, what happened?'

'Some sort of miscalculation, they said. But it worked out in our favour.'

Marian got out of the car and stood beside her father. They looked at their home – Craig's great Australian 'dream-come-true'.

'Congratulations, Dad. All your hard work's paid off. I hope it was worth it.'

* * *

'Mrs Gardiner was magnificent,' Marian said. 'She saved me, Imogen.'

'Don't be ridiculous, Marian. You would have done just fine without me. But I think we made a pretty good team, and I think it's high time you stopped calling me Mrs Gardiner.'

'Well, I suppose we could be a little less formal, seeing as though we'll be spending eternity together,' Marian said with a smile.

The three of them were sitting together by the lake. Marian had gone to talk to Imogen about what she'd seen – about what'd happened – and she'd discovered Mrs Gardiner already there with the same idea in mind.

'It is a good thing that this has happened, for both of you,' Imogen said.

'What do you mean?' Marian said, a shiver running down her spine as she thought of that stone-grey face with its lifeless eyes.

'Well, now I'm convinced that you're not only able to recognise the evil but you are strong enough to overcome it. I'm very proud of you, my dear.'

'I was terrified to tell you the truth but I had my angel with me.' Marian threw a loving glance at Margot.

'And as for you,' Imogen said, turning to Margot, 'you passed *your* first test with flying colours.'

'Thank you, Imogen. Thank you for your faith in me, and for allowing me to watch over her,' she whispered.

'There'll be others – they'll want things from you – they'll try to control you.' Imogen began pacing in front of them with her hands behind her back.

Marian and Margot lost their smiles as the seriousness of the situation began to dawn on them.

'There's as much good as there is evil, existing together but apart, and knowing the difference – feeling it, is everything.' Imogen stopped her pacing, and peered closely into Marian's eyes. 'You seem to have come through the ordeal unharmed. The evil can sometimes leave a little of itself behind.'

'I don't feel any different,' Marian said.

'That may be so, but you're definitely wiser.'

Chapter 12

'I don't think I could lead an ordinary life now, but I do miss ordinary,' Marian said. Margot had been dead to everyone but Marian for over a month now.

'Hmm, I miss life altogether,' Raven said.

'Hey, you've never told me what happened to you exactly. Were you very sick?'

'No, I fell from my horse – remember?'

'That's not what you told me before.'

'Well then, you weren't listening.'

'Maybe I got it wrong – nothing would surprise me at this point.'

Raven nodded, settling back in the balcony chair to tell her story.

'A very long time ago, I was thrown from a horse when I was a little girl. It was a tragic accident but I stayed around for my father's sake.'

Marian tried to forget what she thought she knew about Raven's death as she imagined what life had been like for her. 'So, your mother died having you and you were all your father had left? That's so sad.'

'I sent him on to join his wife when his time came. All he really wanted was to be with her.'

'But he had you – that must have been a comfort?'

Raven shrugged.

'And you didn't go on to your own paradise?' Marian asked.

'I'd met Imogen by then and she sent me to you – to do *this* job. She was the one who made me leave you and she aged my appearance before she sent me back, so we could be friends again. I've seen so many things – been a part of countless lifetimes, but I've never seen anything like you. You're destined for great things, Marian. I want to be a part of that.'

'I don't know about that, Raven – but thank you.'

'So, will you rule the world, or what?'

Which one? Marian thought. Beneath Raven's constant smile, she could detect an edge to her voice sometimes that could cut through steel.

'Can you quit this job? You know – maybe you could do something else other than follow me around all the time?'

'Quit? Why would you say something like that? Didn't you hear what I just said?'

'Oh, I don't know. I get the feeling that you aren't altogether happy. Am I your only client?'

'Client – what are you talking about? I've been assigned to you because you are alive and living in a spiritual world. No-one has ever seen The Magenta Sky before death. We think you're the first; none of us really knows what to expect. I'm here to guide and protect you.'

Marian wasn't convinced. It had sounded like a rehearsed speech – like someone had told her what to say. 'Don't you want to go on to your paradise?' she asked Raven.

'I'll get there, when I'm good and ready.'

Marian caught the twinkle in Raven's eye, like a fiery flash. 'What am I going to do with you?'

'Just hurry up and grow into your greatness, will you? Hey, I like that.'

They both laughed.

'But seriously, Raven, what about your paradise? You'll go there eventually, won't you?'

'You have more choices than I do, Marian.' Then she stood up and floated away without another word.

Marian stayed where she was, thinking about what Raven had said. She wondered about the choices they both had. Sometimes, she felt like she had no choice at all. She looked up, ready to follow Raven but she wandered back inside instead.

She thought about Oliver, her ex-boyfriend, and the way they'd left things. A sigh escaped her lips as she remembered the way he used to look at her. *The only one for me,* Marian thought, remembering the words they had always said to each other. She picked up the phone and saw all the missed calls. She thought about calling him but then remembered why they were apart. A lifetime was a commitment she just wasn't ready to make, no matter how she felt about him.

Marian looked at the pile of papers that'd been awaiting her attention but had been left to gather dust while she'd been soaring through the sky. *I was so excited about this,* she thought as she shuffled through the pile. *All I ever wanted to do was study to be a doctor, now I don't know what to do.* She picked up the syllabus for first semester and looked down the list of subjects for a minute, then tossed it aside. She didn't feel the spark – that excitement she'd always felt at the thought of helping people. Her dream of taking on all the hopeless cases, for saving the day, was gone.

'Can I come in?'

Marian had been so deep in thought, she hadn't heard the tapping on her door.

'Bronte! God, it's good to see you.'

'Well, I got sick of waiting for you to call me back, so here I am,' Bronte said, thinking how terrible her friend looked.

'Yeah, well, I'm sorry about that,' Marian mumbled.

'Been getting ready?' Bronte said when she saw the papers strewn all over the desk.

Marian shook her head.

'I'm just not feeling it anymore. The anticipation's gone.'

'What do you mean? This's all you've *ever* wanted to do.'

'I know, but lately, I've been thinking that there's more to life.' *And death,* Marian thought.

'Like what? Tell me.'

'Something's been happening to me – something strange and wonderful.'

Bronte sat back on the bed, ready to listen.

'No, let's go out on the balcony. It's so much nicer out there,' Marian said.

'Why don't we get out of here altogether. Let's go for coffee.'

They walked down towards the beach, heading for the little café that always had sand on the floor, a fresh breeze blowing through the window and the best coffee.

I can't do this with Raven, Marian thought, as she picked up the menu and searched through the choices. It was a perfect spring day, so they decided to sit outside.

'You look like you've lost weight,' Bronte said.

'Oh, I don't know – maybe.'

'You're so tall and slim, but I think you look a little on the skinny side now.'

I can't remember the last time I was hungry, Marian thought. 'Then I'll order a full-cream latte,' she said.

Bronte laughed. 'So, what's so strange and wonderful?'

'I can see the dead.'

'And I can fly in the air,' Bronte said, a giggle escaping her lips.

'Oh, I can do that too. But it's more of a floating thing, really.'

'Oh my God! You're serious.'

'Deadly.'

'I'm almost afraid to ask but tell me.'

'I thought Mrs Gardiner – Margot – was the first, you know, after she died, but I saw Raven when I was little.'

'And she's dead too?'

'Yes, so she tells me.'

'Well, you're either psychic or psychotic.'

'Or neurotic,' Marian said, a sad smile playing on her lips.

'Who's having the latte?' said the waitress, arriving with the coffee. Bronte pointed to Marian and took the cappuccino for herself.

'I guess we need some help then,' Bronte said, after half her coffee was gone.

'What do you mean, Bronte?'

'I think we need a definitive diagnosis.'

'You're not a doctor yet.'

'Oh, but I will be, and so will you. And right now, we need to find out what's going on.'

'And how do you propose we do that?'

'I've never told you this before, but I believe in the afterlife, you know, spirits – things that go bump in the night – that sort of thing.'

'Oh Bronte! Be serious.'

'But I am. Look over there.' Bronte pointed across the road to a billboard that had an enormous multi-coloured peace sign painted on it. *Body, Mind and Spirit must be in balance* was written underneath it.

'That's new – I haven't seen that before.' Marian rose from the table and wandered across the street. Bronte went inside to pay the bill and then hurried after her.

'There it is. Just down the lane there, see?' Marian turned and pointed straight ahead.

The small shop was a wonder of colour and light. The peace sign was repeated on the shop-front window, as well as the words.

'That's what's wrong with me – an unbalanced mind,' Marian whispered as they opened the door to the tinkling of bells.

'May I help you?' the lady behind the counter said.

Marian hardly heard her as she felt the hairs stand up on the back of her neck. She stared at the beaded curtain that swayed slightly in the wind created by the ceiling fan. She was mesmerised by the movement of the amber beads.

'That's where I do my readings,' the shop owner said, following Marian's gaze. 'My name's Celia.' She came out from behind the counter and extended her hand.

'Nice to meet you,' Bronte said, taking Celia's hand in hers. 'I'm Bronte, and this is Marian.'

Marian still seemed not to hear her. She parted the curtain to one side and went through to the back of the shop. The window on the far wall was open, revealing an ominous dark sky. *Strange,* Marian thought as she watched the storm clouds roll in, *the sun was out a minute ago.* She poked her head through the window thinking how much she loved a good storm – all the fury of nature unleashing itself. But there was no wild wind, no thunder and lightning. There was only a stillness, a quiet that simmered just off the boil, then a spark, and then another, until the window framed nothing but fire.

Marian instinctively backed away from the instant inferno, fearing what was to happen next. Then realising there was no heat, she took a hesitant step forward. She reached out, fascinated by the orange flames and how cool they were to the touch.

A face began to separate itself from the fire, then a body, whose fiery arms flailed around in a grotesque dance. Marian stood enthralled as the fiery body came closer, hypnotising her, keeping her in its sights, before it encircled her in its fiery embrace. It began to pull her through the window. She was powerless to resist as she was swallowed up in the flames. The face aligned itself with Marian's, a cruel challenge reflected in the eyes.

'You will not harm me,' Marian commanded the fiery figure. 'You will let me go – now!' The grip loosened, and then the arms that held her lost their shape as the figure became one again with the fire. The flames began to die back until they were nothing more than a few spitting sparks. Marian watched the light of the last ember go out before she turned and climbed back through the window.

'What were you doing out there?' Bronte said, coming through the curtain in time to catch Marian with her legs over the windowsill.

'You wouldn't believe me if I told you,' Marian said, turning around to look out the window again.

'She mightn't, but I would,' Celia said, shuffling a deck of tarot cards. She sat down at a little table in the middle of the room. 'Here, Marian. Sit down.'

But Marian wasn't listening; she had her head stuck out the window again. All traces of the fire had gone. There were no storm clouds darkening the horizon and the sun had returned with its brilliance, covering the scene with light.

Now, there was an old soldier out there. The sun glinted off the row of medals on his chest. He stood quietly, looking at Celia.

'Can I help you? Are you okay?' Marian said. *Did he come from the fire?* she thought.

'I'm sorry about that fire. That creature was too quick for me,' the soldier said. 'Oh, and you can see me?' His old blue eyes crinkled at the corners, animating his face.

'Yes, I can. Who are you?'

'Allow me to introduce myself: I'm Heston, Celia's grandfather.'

'I'll just let Celia know you're here.' Marian pulled her head back inside and turned to the others. Bronte was staring, afraid for Marian, while Celia sat at the table, shuffling the tarot cards.

'Celia, your grandfather's here,' Marian said quietly.

Celia put the cards down carefully on the table and looked blankly at Marian. 'What did you say?'

'It's Heston – he's here.'

Celia's hand flew to her mouth as she choked back a sob. 'It can't be – I can't believe it.'

'That's his name, right? I can describe him to you, if you like.'

'No, no, I believe you. It's such a miracle that you can see him.'

'I don't understand – you know he's here?'

'Yes, but I can't *see* him. I'd give anything to have a gift like yours.'

Marian shook her head, thinking of the fiery figure. *God knows what it would have done with me if I hadn't scared it off,* she thought. 'I haven't decided how I feel about it all yet. I don't know if it's such a good thing or not. I'm still grappling with the whole concept.' She stole a quick look out the window but she saw nothing menacing, just the proud, old soldier standing to attention at his post.

Celia went to the window. She looked out at the sunny day which had suddenly become so much brighter for her. She was comforted by the thought that her grandfather was out there. 'You could help people – all sorts of people from all sorts of places,' she said, turning to Marian with tears glistening in her eyes. 'We could accomplish so much together with a talent like yours,' Celia said, imagining all the good they could do.

'I thought that's what you were all about,' Bronte said, 'helping people who really need it – champion of the lost causes. We might even have a diagnosis here.'

'Oh, I don't know,' Marian said. 'This's a long way from uni.'

'If you're helping people, does it really matter how?' Bronte said.

'I can't help anyone until I help myself. I need a second opinion.'

Chapter 13

Marian swirled her feet through the magenta water. After the encounters at Celia's shop, she needed a break. She could feel the peace settle over her immediately. Real or not, this place was her haven. The people were happy here in their purpose of transition, their gentle busyness bubbling away as they set their affairs in order.

As she glanced around the lake's rim, she noticed a young man with a troubled look on his face. He was pacing up and down by the water's edge while Mina chased after him. He seemed so out of place.

'But I can't be dead,' Marian heard him say. 'I can't be – I'm not – this is just a bad dream.' *This may be a dream, but it's not a bad one,* Marian thought, as she pulled her feet from the water and stood up. She glided across the ground towards him, her eyes luminous with a sparkling glow.

The young man looked up as she came closer. He stopped his frantic pacing and stood completely still, watching Marian approach.

'Henry,' Marian said softly, 'we need to talk.' She touched his arm lightly and all signs of trouble left his face. They sat down by the water's edge and Marian held his hand. *Everyone's here for a reason,* she thought. Marian was drawn to him – she wanted to help him find his way. 'Henry, I know this feels impossible to believe right now but you have just passed away.' The young man's face remained blank as he continued to stare at her. 'Henry, you're dead.'

'That can't be! Look at all these people – look at this place. And how do you know my name?'

'I know everything about you,' Marian said, gazing into the depths of his eyes and seeing his life and death unfolding before her. She led him to the lake's rim and they sat and talked until Henry began to understand.

Mina stood by, watching Marian work her magic with this newly dead soul until she could see he had accepted his death, and then she led him away.

'You were wonderful with him, Marian,' Imogen said. 'Mina should be able to take things from here.'

Marian thought about what she had just said to Henry. 'The words came easily – I knew just what to say.'

'And that's why your work here will become so important.'

'I could see what happened to him, Imogen. I saw the hospital bed, the doctors, his family, and the enormous crowd spilling from the church at the funeral.'

'He's young – he wasn't ready. His soul's in shock from its sudden rip from life.'

'Is that why he's here?'

'I imagine so. He only needs some time – unless there *are* other reasons.'

'He just kept saying he wanted to go home. I explained to him that he's on his way there.' Marian mused about the *real* reasons why this young man was taken so soon.

'It's a sub-conscious decision we make, to come and go. Our soul knows what it wants – what is needed for it to grow and survive,' Imogen explained.

'Yes, there's no real death.' Marian thought she understood that now. *But death, or not, I still have my life to live,* she thought.

'Yes, you'll have to find a way to combine the two,' Imogen said, smiling at Marian's stunned expression. Then she nodded and kissed Marian lightly on the cheek. It was almost imperceptible, but Marian felt her touch. She placed her hand where the warm kiss still lingered and marvelled that she could *feel* the dead.

'There are things you've begun that you need to finish,' Imogen said.

Marian thought about the university degree that had been so important to her before Margot had died and had begun to appear to her. Since then, she'd thought of nothing else but this new world. Oliver was almost gone from her thoughts completely. She tried to see him in her mind's eye, but he was just a fuzzy picture now.

'But I'm still not sure if all this is real.'

'My dear, what does *real* mean anyway?'

'I guess it's an individual perception.'

'I'm real, you know,' Raven said, who'd wandered over from the other side of the lake.

'Where've you been?' Imogen said, her eyes narrowing. 'You know you need my permission to leave.'

'I was at the hospital – you know, seeing if there was anything I could do.'

'That's very commendable, Raven, but your place is with Marian. And you, Marian – you've got a lot of thinking to do.'

'You seem so real,' Marian said, touching Raven's arm as they glided through the clouds.

'I *am* real, silly,' she said, reaching through the white fluff to poke Marian in the ribs.

'Well, you would say that, wouldn't you? No self-respecting delusion would lie now, would it?' They both began to giggle, and by the time Marian's feet touched the tiles on her balcony, she was laughing so loudly that Sonia and Craig could hear her over the movie they were watching in the lounge room.

* * *

'Listen to that! I haven't heard her laugh like that in a long time,' Craig said.

'What could she be laughing at?'

'She must be on the phone.'

'I guess so, but she sounds almost hysterical. I think I'll go and see if everything's alright.'

Sonia knocked on Marian's door but the laughter on the other side drowned out any chance of her being heard, so she opened it cautiously and peeked inside. She found Marian rolling around on the bed, tears streaming down her face.

'Marian, for God's sake, what are you laughing at?' The TV was off and the phone was nowhere to be seen.

'Oh, just something Raven said.' Marian sat up and wiped the tears from her eyes, the serious look on Sonia's face dispelling her mirth.

'I just don't understand what's wrong with you. I thought you were getting better. I thought you were okay,' her mother said.

'But I *am* okay, and if you'd just open your eyes – open your mind – you'd see it for yourself.'

'My mind's plenty open, thank you very much. *You're* the one who seems to be going out of hers.' Without another word, Sonia turned and fled the room. *I shouldn't have said that,* she thought. She ran down the stairs, almost tripping over herself in her haste.

'We have to do something,' Sonia said, standing in front of the TV and blocking Craig's view.

'What are you talking about? Do something about what?' Craig said.

'This Raven thing has gone far enough. She needs help, Craig.'

'Here, come and sit down.'

'I don't want to sit down. I want you to listen to me.'

'And I want you both to listen to *me,*' Marian said, flying through the door, her eyes flashing with anger. 'Raven is real – you need to believe me.'

'I think *you* believe it,' Sonia began, 'even though the idea is ridiculous.'

'How would you know? You're afraid of your own shadow.'

'This isn't about me, Marian. I'm not the one talking to myself.'

'Now, you two, this isn't going to get us anywhere,' Craig said, jumping in before either of them said anything they'd regret.

'You tell her, Craig. Tell her this has got to stop,' Sonia said, turning to her husband.

'It may not be as simple as that. We might have to get some help.'

'Finally – finally you're listening to me,' Sonia said.

'Yes, I think we need an expert.'

'So now you're branding me with the crazy stamp, is that it?' Marian said.

'I didn't say what kind of help, did I?'

Oh God! No – not that, Sonia thought, dreading what was coming. 'I want to take her to a doctor, Craig. Not someone like your mother.'

'What do you mean, Mum? What about Dad's mum?'

'You would have adored my mother. I've always seen her in you,' Craig said, his eyes misting over.

'I would have loved to have met her,' Marian said, looking at the picture on the bookshelf of a woman taken too soon.

'Yes, she was amazing.' Craig picked up the photo with a wistful smile. There was always a house full of people when he was growing up. People came from far and wide to see his mother and seek her counsel. She taught Craig to keep an open mind and embrace all of life's experiences. 'Maybe you're more like her than I thought.'

'Now *you're* being ridiculous. Your mother was lovely – don't get me wrong – but she had her head in the clouds.'

'There's no point in getting into the same old argument, Sonia,' Craig said, throwing his hands up in the air. 'We'll never agree on this but Marian deserves the chance to make up her own mind.'

'She needs to see a doctor, Craig,' Sonia said, folding her arms across her chest. 'There's something wrong with her.'

'That's Marian's decision – it's up to her,' Craig said.

Marian looked from one to the other. 'I think I'll go for a walk. I've got a lot to think about.'

* * *

'That didn't go too well,' Raven said. She was standing on the shore with her feet in the shallow water.

'I don't want to talk about it. Could you just leave me alone for a while?'

'I think we need to work out what we're going to do next,' Raven said.

'*We* – don't you mean me?'

'You know what Imogen said – where you go, I go.'

And she doesn't look so happy about it either, Marian thought, catching the fleeting look of annoyance on Raven's face before she rearranged it back to its usual smile.

Marian sat down at the water's edge, letting the water ripple over her feet.

'I guess this's it. You'll have to decide one way or the other,' Raven said.

'You mean, if I have a gift or I'm possessed by a curse?'

* * *

Sonia and Craig were watching from a safe distance. They'd followed Marian down to the beach, just to make sure she was okay.

'See, she's talking to herself again,' Sonia said. 'What're we going to do?'

Craig watched Marian interact with the empty space on her left. 'I wish I knew what she was saying,' he said.

'What difference would that make?'

'Well, it might give us a clue as to how to handle this.'

'We don't know how to handle this – that's the problem. We can't even agree on who she should see.' Sonia wasn't as open-minded as her husband. She only believed in what she could see with her own eyes. She needed a rational explanation and scientific proof. However, Craig believed in everything – aliens, spirits and magic, and most of all, his daughter.

'We'll suggest a doctor first but if he can find nothing wrong with her, then I think we should help her to explore other avenues.'

Sonia nodded, already imagining what the doctor would say. She was so glad this was out in the open but she didn't want to hear any more talk about psychics. It made her nervous. She looked back towards the water to where Marian was standing. The sun was in her eyes now and she had to shade them so she could see what her daughter was doing. For a minute, Sonia thought she saw Marian floating above the water. *This is really starting to get to me*, she thought.

Chapter 14

'It's so good to see you,' Lisa said when she opened her front door and saw Marian standing there. She grabbed her, hugging her tight. 'I've been really worried about you.'

'I've just been driving around and here I am, I guess. Therese isn't home.'

'What's wrong? You're shaking all over.' Lisa released her grip on Marian and stepped back so she could get a good look at her.

'They want me to see a doctor,' Marian said.

'Well, surely you can see why – especially considering how your mother is.' *And screaming out to the world that you can fly didn't help either,* Lisa thought.

'I know, but she doesn't listen to me.'

'Let's go up to my room where we can talk.'

On the way to Lisa's room, Marian stopped on the landing. The window halfway up gave her a full view of Therese's back yard. 'The trees are gone … look, Lisa.' Marian felt a deep sense of loss as she viewed the large, almost barren yard. The only tree left was the one that held the treehouse and it stood determined and alone, swaying slightly in the breeze. A wistful smile lifted the corners of Marian's mouth as she thought of all the secrets that lone tree held in its branches.

Lisa watched the sadness cross Marian's face like an afternoon shadow. *She's not right,* she thought, as she noticed the shadow darken. 'Are you alright?' Lisa said, propelling Marian into her room. 'Do you want to talk about it?' Lisa handed Marian a tissue and watched the distress play on her friend's face.

'Either way, everything's changed for me,' Marian said. 'I can never have my nice, neat, ordered life again.'

'What about Oliver?'

'What's he got to do with this?' Marian eyed Lisa suspiciously. 'Have you been talking to him?'

Lisa shook her head. 'You two were so close for nearly a year, Marian, and then it was suddenly over.'

'I told you, we were getting *too* close. I needed some space.'

'Okay, okay, but you must miss him.'

Marian thought about the guy who'd stolen her heart – who still had it, but he had wanted more from her – more than she was willing to give.

'I think I'll see if Therese is home yet,' Marian said, changing the subject. 'I think I heard her car.'

'Okay,' Lisa said, walking her to the front door. 'I hope you feel better soon.'

Marian wandered off down the path to the front gate. She turned to wave goodbye to Lisa, but she'd already gone back inside. She looked hard at the door, willing herself to see through it, but it remained solid and heavy.

When she reached the end of the path, she turned around and looked at Lisa's door again. The dark brown wood seemed to shimmer, and as Marian continued to stare, it became as translucent as a pane of glass. Marian could see straight through it to Lisa talking on the phone. She was sure Lisa was blabbing to Therese. *I don't need any special talent to figure that out,* she thought.

'Why did you cut the trees down?' Marian said to her aunt the second she opened the door. She choked back a sob. 'I loved those trees.'

'Come inside, honey. Please don't upset yourself like this.'

Marian strode through the house and out the back door. The backyard was like a foreign landscape with the trees gone. It was almost stripped bare. Marian stood at the bottom of the only one left and looked up into its branches.

'Thanks for not chopping this one down, even though you probably thought you should after the scene I created up there the other day.'

'I have to admit I thought about it, but I couldn't bring myself to destroy the treehouse. You aren't going to try and use it for a launching pad again or anything are you?'

'No, I think my flying days are over.' Marian looked up at the treehouse. 'I'm so glad it's still there. That treehouse means a lot to me – to us.'

'Yes, our childhood playhouse.'

The two of them shaded their eyes against the afternoon sun, looking skywards. Therese thought she saw something moving around in the treehouse. She squinted hard against the sun and looked again, but whatever it was, had disappeared.

'Do you want to go up?' Marian said, her hand already on the first branch of the tree.

'No!' Therese said. 'I mean, let's go inside. I need some water.'

'They want to take me to see a doctor,' Marian said when they were safely in the kitchen. 'Maybe I've got a brain tumour or something.'

'Don't say that. We just need to make sure you're okay. You haven't been to the doctor since you were little. In fact, you've never really been sick a day in your life.'

'I remember getting lollipops if I didn't cry when I had my needles.'

'We'll get to the bottom of this. You'll see – you'll be fine,' Therese said, while wondering if she herself would ever be fine again. She felt her hands trembling.

'But I'm not – either way, I'm not. There's this whole other world out there – up there – that I'm a part of now.' Marian gazed out the window. 'I really can fly,' she whispered.

Marian got up from the kitchen table. Therese half-expected her to fly out the back door but instead, she walked purposely down the hall and out to her car.

'Please don't worry about me too much, Therese,' Marian called out to her aunt who stood by the front door. 'Like you said, we'll get to the bottom of this.'

Chapter 15

Marian looked for her own doctor. She didn't want to go to the one Sonia went to. She didn't want her mother to have any influence in any way. *Maybe I can pick the right one if I look at this list long enough,* Marian thought, studying the names listed on a sign on the old building. In the end, she chose Dr Emery. Not for any special reason – she just felt drawn to the name.

'May I help you?' the receptionist said, smiling pleasantly at Marian from behind the desk.

Marian was about to answer when she felt a slight tugging on her skirt. She looked down to see a little boy – the same little boy who'd stood at the end of her bed trying to talk to her. She could feel a warmth radiating from him. He smiled as he slipped his little hand in hers.

'Are you alright, Miss?' the receptionist said, the smile changing to a slight frown.

'Oh, yes, I'm sorry,' Marian said, tearing her eyes away from the cute little boy. 'I'd like to make an appointment with Dr Emery, if that's possible.'

The little boy nodded enthusiastically and skipped away to the corner of the room. *I've come to the right place,* Marian thought, fascinated by the tiny space between his little feet and the tiles on the floor as he hovered slightly in the air.

'Have you seen the doctor before?' the receptionist asked.

'Ah, no, I haven't seen *any* doctor since I was a little girl.'

The receptionist lowered her head and got busy on the computer. 'Actually, there's been a cancellation for later this afternoon. Would that be suitable?'

* * *

While she waited for her appointment time, Marian wandered around the nearby mall, wracking her brains trying to decide what she was going to say to the doctor. The truth – her truth – sounded like a made-up story. The only thing that gave her courage was the trusting look she'd seen in the eyes of that little boy in the doctor's surgery. She decided she shouldn't see the doctor alone so she headed to the parking lot to fetch her car. Her logical mind won over her emotional state as she drove home to tell her mother.

'I've decided to see a GP and see what he's got to say about me,' Marian said as she broke the news to Sonia.

'I'm so pleased. You've made the right decision. I'll get you the number for mine.'

'No need – I already have an appointment.'

'With who?'

'*My* doctor. I found my own but I'd like you to come with me.'

'Of course.'

'Now, you're to let me do all the talking, Mum,' Marian said, knowing her mother would struggle to keep her mouth shut. 'The appointment's in an hour.'

'I'd better call your father. He'll want to be there too. '

* * *

'Welcome – please take a seat,' Dr Emery said, closing the old oak door behind them. He took up his position behind his antique desk and looked expectantly at the three of them seated before him. 'How may I help you today?'

Marian liked him immediately. He had kind eyes and she felt as though she could trust him. His office felt safe with its old-world charm. She stole a sideways glance at her parents. She was comforted by Craig's presence but Sonia looked as though she'd rather be anywhere else. *Well, she wanted this,* Marian thought.

There was an awkward silence as the little group struggled to begin.

'So, Mum's worried about me,' Marian said, determined to get the appointment started.

'My wife has some serious concerns about our daughter,' Craig said, earning a scathing look from Sonia. 'She feels her behaviour's out of her usual character.'

Dr Emery picked up his pen. 'How so?' he said, looking directly at Sonia.

'Well, she's just not herself,' Sonia said. 'She's seeing things – hearing things – I don't know what to do with her.'

So much for keeping her mouth shut, Marian thought.

'What have you got to say about that, Marian?' Dr Emery said gently.

Marian began to feel uncomfortable as everyone waited for her answer. She didn't really want to be here and now they were all putting her on the spot.

'This was all Mum's idea. There's nothing wrong with me.' Marian crossed her arms tightly across her chest, preparing to do battle. Marian had gone along with this doctor thing to get Sonia off her back but she'd be damned if she'd lie. She was learning to trust her instincts and they were telling her that everything would be alright. She didn't need to pretend.

'Marian, would you mind stepping outside for just a moment?' Dr Emery said. 'I just want a quick word with your parents.'

'Yes, I would mind. I'm almost a grown woman.'

'Please, Marian,' Craig said, his eyes pleading with her.

Same old story – Mum gets her own way, Marian thought, resisting the temptation to slam the door on her way out.

* * *

Dr Emery gave Sonia and Craig his full attention. He noted the anger in her and the fear in him. 'Now, please explain the concerns you have with your daughter.'

'Maybe we've made a mistake,' Craig said, rushing in before Sonia had a chance to reply.

'I can't do this all by myself,' Sonia said. 'We agreed she needs help – remember?' Sonia glared at Craig. She knew they'd fight about this later but she needed to concentrate on Marian right now. 'It all started when she was a little girl …'

* * *

Marian was sitting just outside but she could hear and see everything that was going on. She heard Sonia trying to explain herself to the doctor. *She's the one who needs a psychiatrist, not me,* Marian thought, listening to Sonia's ravings. She could see Dr Emery making notes and nodding his head from time to time.

'We may need to refer Marian to a psychiatrist,' Dr Emery said when Sonia had finished telling him her story, 'just to cover all the bases.'

She almost looks happy, Marian thought, as she saw the smug look replace the anger on Sonia's face.

'However, I'd like to run some tests to rule out any organic causes first.'

'Organic causes?' Craig said.

'Yes, there may be other reasons to account for her change in behaviour,' Dr Emery said. 'But I'll need to talk to her before we go any further.'

Marian watched the doctor rise from his chair and stride purposely to the office door.

'Marian, could you join us please?'

Marian tried to arrange a bland look on her face to hide the seething emotions she was feeling.

'I have a few questions for you,' Dr Emery said. His voice was so kind and his manner so reassuring, that Marian's anger evaporated.

'Alright,' Marian said, 'but could I ask you one first?'

'Surely – anything you like.'

'Do you always bring your son to work with you?'

'See, this's exactly what I'm talking about,' Sonia said. 'She doesn't make any sense.'

'Mrs White – could you please refrain from interrupting?'

'Yes, Sonia, be quiet,' Craig said.

Sonia shut her mouth as quickly as she had opened it. She sat back, ready to watch the show, thinking how interesting it would be to see how these two know-it-alls would handle the situation.

'I'm not sure I understand what you mean, Marian,' Dr Emery said.

'It doesn't matter,' Marian mumbled. 'What did you want to ask me?'

'Oh, I was going to ask if you've experienced any headaches, nausea, dizziness or sleeping difficulties?'

Marian shook her head. *I don't sleep at all,* she thought, thinking of her nights up in The Magenta Sky. *Being there refreshes me more than any amount of sleep ever could.*

'What about your memory – any problems with that?'

Not if you don't count its awakening, Marian thought, shaking her head again.

Dr Emery scribbled on his notepad for a moment.

'Do you think I've got a brain tumour?' Marian said, watching him carefully. He looked so uncomfortable.

'I think we should do some tests – just to be sure.'

'You're the doctor.' Marian shrugged her shoulders and leant back in her chair. A sudden movement caught her eye, like a patch of exploding colour in a night sky. A cheeky face peeked out from behind Dr Emery's chair and grinned at her. It was the little boy again. Marian watched him in wonder. *Well, if I'm delusional or hallucinating, at least I'm consistent.* She resisted the urge to smile back.

Chapter 16

Seeing the doctor hadn't been what Marian had expected. She couldn't decide if she felt better or worse. She studied the referrals in her hand and made notes in her diary of the appointments. CT scans – psychiatrists – it was all a bit much.

Marian hardly spoke to Sonia on the way home, thinking about her mother's dramatic performance for Dr Emery's benefit and how she always managed to make it about her. *God help her if there's really something wrong with me.* Marian wondered about the little boy – who he was and if he was alright.

'So how did it go?' Raven said, blowing in through the balcony door.

'I'm sure I don't have to tell you how it went,' Marian said. 'I'm sure you already know.'

Marian pushed past her onto the balcony and leant on the railing. She took a few deep breaths and let the salt air fill her lungs.

'You know what, Raven? I've had enough of this for a while. I think I'll go for a swim … on my own.'

The weather was still a little cool. Spring had barely begun but Marian felt the familiar thrill at the thought of her first swim of the season.

* * *

Sonia saw Marian leave with her pink, striped beach towel over her shoulder.

'You don't think it's too cold for a swim?' Sonia called from the front door but Marian ignored her, walking purposely towards the ocean.

I hope she comes back in a better mood, Sonia thought, wondering if she should follow.

'Craig, Marian's gone to the beach,' Sonia called out to her husband who was in the lounge room.

'She probably just needs some space. She'll come back when she's had it,' Craig said, switching on the TV.

Still at the front door, Sonia hummed to herself as she thought about the success of the day. *She'll get the help she needs now,* she thought, as she watched the pink towel disappear around the corner. She almost skipped into the kitchen where she opened the fridge and reached in for the vegetables, back to the safety of her comforting routine.

* * *

The ocean was beautiful – not too choppy – a perfect afternoon to be in the water. Marian took off her dress and folded her towel neatly on top of it. As she swam out through the waves, she felt buoyed by the ocean. She felt strong and confident as she stretched her body to its limits. After a while, she rolled over onto her back and stared up at the blue sky. She watched the seagulls hover above her as she floated in a sea of peace.

Marian suddenly realised she'd lost track of what was going on with the ocean – something her father warned her never to do. Craig had been a lifesaver on the beach when he was young and he'd drummed into Marian the importance of water safety. She rolled back onto her stomach and looked towards the shore.

It was only a speck in the distance now. She began to swim towards it but she could feel the current pulling against her.

Marian was caught in a rip. She couldn't get back in and it was pulling her further out to sea. She knew not to panic and to go with the current until she could escape it, then swim back to safety. This wasn't the first time she'd been caught like this but she'd never experienced such a menacing pull before. It felt like a thousand hands were grabbing at her, trying to drag her out and under. She tried treading water but soon grew tired. She turned over on her back to float for a while so she could rest.

The sky began to change colour. It was getting dark. Marian turned her head sideways and stared at the magenta-coloured fingers creeping out from the horizon. *It's so pretty,* she thought, as she went under the water and then came up, coughing and spluttering.

'Raven!' she screamed, her mouth filling with water as she went under again.

* * *

Sonia frowned at the wall clock in the kitchen. *She's been gone almost two hours,* she thought. She poked her head into the lounge room where Craig was glued to the TV.

'Craig – could you please go and see what's taking Marian so long? She should be back by now.'

'You mean she's still at the beach?' He glanced out the window at the lengthening shadows. He was out of the chair in an instant.

'Could you tell her that dinner won't be long? Tell her to come home,' Sonia said.

But Craig didn't hear her. He was already out the front door.

* * *

Craig ran down to the beach, hoping to find Marian on her way back but he could find no sign of her. He thought she must have gone for a walk until he noticed the pink, striped beach towel on the sand. He felt his heart hammer in his chest as he tore down to the water's edge, desperately scanning the ocean for any sign of her. His experienced eye could see the rip and he followed its course out to sea. *There's something out there – way out there,* he thought.

He ripped off his shirt, kicked the shoes from his feet and threw himself into the water. Just before he dived under the waves, the tiny blimp he had in his sights began to move. It rose above the water, above the waves, and glided towards the shore.

Craig stood completely still, letting the waves wash over him as he kept the object directly in his sights. *My God, it's her,* he thought, as the object came close enough for him to recognise his daughter. He stole a look to his left and right but realised he was the sole witness to this impossible phenomenon. His open mind split in two as he tried to comprehend what was happening – what he was seeing. The only thing that kept him from falling apart was the knowledge that Marian was somehow coming to safety.

She was about twenty metres from the shore when her body lost its levitation and plummeted straight down, disappearing into the swell of white water.

Craig snapped out of his trance and threw himself into the surf to rescue her. He dived under the waves, surfacing a minute later with Marian in his arms. He carried her limp body to the shore and laid her on the sand. She wasn't breathing. He couldn't find a pulse. His lifesaving training kicked in and after a few minutes of CPR, he got a pulse, and some of the colour returned to her pale face. Marian was breathing on her own but she was unconscious.

Craig grabbed his shirt, fumbled in the pocket for his phone and dialled emergency. A few minutes later, the wail of a siren brought Craig a measure of reassurance. Sonia, alerted by the noise and a sick feeling in her stomach that it may have something to do with her family, arrived just before the ambulance.

'My God. What's happened?' Sonia screamed, clutching Marian's limp hand and scrutinising her face for signs of life.

'She nearly drowned,' Craig said, never taking his eyes off Marian's face.

'What? But she's such a good swimmer. Marian, Marian, wake up,' Sonia begged, cradling her daughter in her arms.

'She's unconscious, Sonia. She can't hear you.'

'But she *has* to hear me. She *has* to wake up!'

* * *

They both rode in the back of the ambulance to the hospital with Marian. The paramedic didn't have the heart to tell them that only one parent was allowed. He didn't like the look of this young patient, so he thought he could make an exception this one time.

When they arrived at the hospital, the emergency staff were waiting to whisk Marian away. Sonia and Craig were shown where to wait with the promise of regular updates on Marian's condition. They sat there together, lost in their disbelief.

'She's such a good swimmer,' Sonia kept repeating to herself, rocking back and forth in the waiting room chair.

Craig just sat and stared ahead. He dared himself to think about what he'd seen down by the water's edge. *She saved herself – otherwise she'd be dead right now,* his fevered mind repeated over and over.

'Mr and Mrs White?' a doctor said, standing in the doorway. Only a few minutes had passed, but it seemed like an eternity for the distraught parents waiting for news.

'Yes Doctor,' Craig said, jumping to his feet and dragging Sonia to hers.

'We have Marian stabilised but she's still unconscious. We're sending her to the intensive care unit.'

Chapter 17

Marian opened her eyes. Everything was a blur but she had a sense of faces looking down on her. And a pink light. She tried to focus on what was in front of her. She lifted her hand and stared at it; she could almost see straight through it. Marian concentrated on the rest of her body and noticed how light it felt, as if it was made of air.

'How do you feel?' a voice said close to her ear. Marian tried harder to focus on the blurry objects around her and as the fog in her mind cleared, the objects became people. She could see the concern and the love on all their faces.

'She's almost with us,' Imogen announced to the hushed figures.

Marian reached out her hand and Imogen took it in hers. Marian could feel the warmth there, but there was something else, like a spark or a tingle, that seemed to kick-start her back to life.

'What happened? How did I get here?' Marian said, trying to sit up.

'You are safe, my dear. Just rest now and give yourself a moment,' Imogen said.

'I wanted to go for a swim. Yes, that's right; I went down to the beach.'

'Yes, you did,' Raven said.

'Shush, Raven,' Imogen warned. 'Marian needs a little peace and quiet right now.'

Marian tried to think but she was distracted by this amazing feeling of euphoria in her body. It pulsated through every cell of her being. *I've never felt more alive,* she thought. Then it hit her – the rip – going under the waves.

'I'm dead, aren't I?' Marian said, absorbing the concern on the ring of faces around her. 'I mean, my body's gone.' She was still holding Imogen's hand as she let herself be pulled into a sitting position. The Magenta Sky was all around, a living colour infusing her body with life. The little group stood quietly waiting for her. There was such a buzz in the air, it almost made a sound. Marian focused on Raven's face, not missing the look she exchanged with Imogen. She saw the raised eyebrows and the subtle nod of the head.

'Your body's in hospital – unconscious,' Raven said, after she received the silent permission to continue.

'Then, how can I be here?'

'That's the question. This is new. Wonderful and new.'

Marian remembered the feeling of the water covering her face and her struggle to release herself from the pull of the rip. Then the renewed determination as she felt her father's anguish emitting from the shore.

'So you lifted yourself out of danger and you went to him,' Imogen said, helping Marian put the pieces together.

'They must be out of their minds with worry,' Marian said, realising with growing horror the extent of the situation now. 'What should I do?'

'Only you can answer that question,' Imogen said. 'At this moment, you exist in both places. You are alive there and living here. This is amazing beyond words, my dear.'

'I want to see,' Marian pleaded, squeezing Imogen's hand. 'I need to see where I am.'

'All you need do is close your eyes and it will all be there, right in front of you.'

Marian closed her eyes tightly. The vision was slow and gradual. After a long moment, she could see herself lying on a hospital bed, hooked up to monitors that buzzed and flashed. Sonia and Craig sat on opposite sides of the bed, holding her hands. Nurses fussed around the machines, muttering words of comfort as they went efficiently about the business of keeping her alive.

'The doctor said there's a good chance she'll wake up,' Marian heard her father say. 'We just have to be patient.'

Marian saw her mother nodding desperately. 'I know she will – of course she will.'

'Look at them, Imogen,' Marian said, her eyes still closed. 'This isn't right.' Marian opened her eyes, tears escaping from behind the closed lids. 'Can you see them?'

The little group nodded in unison.

'Yes, we can,' Raven said, placing her arm gently around Marian's shoulder. Raven needed Marian to stay in The Magenta Sky; she needed her to stay for her plan to work.

'I have to go back, I can't leave them like this,' Marian told the others.

'But what about what you want – what I want?' Raven said, snatching her arm away.

'What do you mean? Look at them!'

But Raven didn't want to look. She turned her back on Marian – on all of them. Her plan wasn't working.

The little group knew what was coming as they stepped back to give Marian some space. She closed her eyes again and vanished as quietly and as suddenly as she'd come.

* * *

'Look, Craig,' Sonia said. 'I think she's waking up.'

They both leaned over their daughter and watched her eyes flutter open. She'd come back to them.

'I'll inform Dr Anderson,' a nurse said from the end of the bed.

Marian woke up for the second time since her near-drowning with a mind empty of memory again.

'Dr Anderson said when she wakes up, she'll probably be very disorientated and she may not remember the accident at all,' Sonia whispered, watching the confusion settle in Marian's eyes.

'What's going on?' Marian said through her oxygen mask. She ripped it off her face and threw it onto the bed.

'No, leave it on, love,' Craig said, retrieving it and gently placing it back over Marian's nose and mouth.

The doctor arrived and examined Marian. 'So, how do you feel, young lady?' he said, putting his stethoscope back in the pocket of his white coat.

'Where's Raven?' Marian said, pulling the mask off again.

'Raven's not real,' Sonia said, the exasperation in her voice distracting the doctor from his patient.

'What're you talking about? I saw her, just a minute ago,' Marian said.

'No, Marian, you didn't. You nearly drowned today. You've been unconscious for almost eleven hours.'

'Marian needs her rest, Mrs White,' the doctor said firmly. 'We can discuss this later.'

'Yes, Sonia – now's not the time,' Craig said, dragging Sonia away from Marian's bedside.

I'm too tired to argue, Marian thought. She felt the warmth and the safety envelop her as she drifted back off to sleep. She dreamt about Raven and a pretty pink place above the sky.

Chapter 18

'You've had a harrowing experience,' Dr Maine, the psychiatrist said, taking up his position at the end of Marian's bed. 'How are you feeling?'

It was the next morning and Marian had opened her eyes to realise it had brought no further clarity with it. Her mind was still muddled and she still couldn't understand what had happened.

Dr Maine checked her vital signs, picked up her chart and made a few entries. 'Dr Anderson asked me to have a look at you. Do you feel up to talking?'

Marian nodded and tried to sit up. The world tilted on its axis for a minute but the dizziness soon passed. Dr Maine plumped her pillows up and sat down on the edge of the bed.

'I can't remember what happened,' Marian said.

'You may suffer some confusion – amnesia – following the accident.'

'I remember needing some space. I went down to the beach but the rest is just a blur.'

'That's a start. It may take some time for it all to come back to you.'

'I'm not sure I want to remember, after what Dad told me.'

'Hmm, I'm more interested in what your mother said.'

'Oh, you mean about Raven?'

'Well, yes, among other things.'

'So I guess you're the psychiatrist, then?'

'Do you mind very much?' After speaking with her mother yesterday, he thought Marian was too young to be this troubled. 'Everything we discuss is strictly confidential. You are very nearly an adult. I see from your chart that you'll be eighteen in a few weeks, so everything is *your* business. The hospital was forced to run a battery of tests when you were admitted due to the critical condition you presented with.'

'Let me guess – they all came back negative – no brain tumours or anything?'

Dr Maine shook his head. 'We'll talk and we'll find your memory. It's in there somewhere.' He tapped Marian's temple gently, patting her on the shoulder with his other hand. 'We'll start with the intricacies of the mind and the deep space of unconsciousness–'

Sonia burst into the room, followed closely by Craig. 'How are you feeling, sweetheart?' she said. She recognised the psychiatrist from their talk yesterday. 'Good morning, Dr Maine.'

'I feel okay. Still lots of blank spaces, but okay. Don't worry, Mum, I know he's the shrink. No offence, Doctor.'

'None taken, Marian. We'll talk later.' Dr Maine got up and offered the space on the bed to Sonia.

'Oh, please don't leave on our account.' Sonia suddenly seemed to remember Craig's existence as he stood awkwardly to one side.

'I'll see you later Marian – Mr and Mrs White.' Dr Maine strode from the room.

Craig sat himself on the edge of the bed, leaving Sonia to stare after the psychiatrist.

'For God's sake, Sonia! It's patient confidentiality.'

'So what? She's my daughter. I have a right to know.'

'She's *our* daughter and it's up to *her* what she wants to tell us.'

'Oh. I'm sure you don't want to know about it anyway. You're probably hoping she has some kind of special gift or something, aren't you?'

Before Craig had a chance to say anything, the door opened. 'What's going on here?' Therese said from behind a huge bunch of flowers. 'Marian doesn't need this.'

'Shut up! Just stop talking – all of you,' Marian said. 'I'm tired. Can you all just go?'

A nurse hurried into the room, alerted by Marian's raised voice. 'You need to step outside while I attend to the patient,' she said.

Craig ushered the two women from the room.

After the nurse left, Marian rolled over onto her side and stared at the wall. Silent tears rolled down her face as she wished she was anywhere but here. *I've never felt so alone,* she thought. Then she felt a gentle touch on her shoulder. She rolled over to see Therese hovering over her.

'I had to come back,' she said. 'I left the others at the coffee shop.'

'Do you think that we choose our own parents?' Marian said, sitting up. Therese sat down on the edge of the bed and took her hand.

'Yes, I think so. I think we pick them to learn the lessons we need to but also to teach them what they need to know as well. I think we all strive for complete compatibility.'

'That makes sense. I could teach Mum so much; she doesn't believe in anything.'

'Your mother's just afraid. Frightened of what she can't see.'

'She's scared of her own shadow, I'm sure.'

'Well, you have to accept her the way she is, the same as I have. She wasn't much fun to grow up with, I can tell you.'

No wonder Mina turned up in her life, Marian thought.

'But she has her good points and she loves you with all her heart,' Therese said.

'I love her too but she makes it hard sometimes.' Marian thought about all the reasons she might have chosen Sonia as her mother. 'I picked her to show her how to open her mind. But she keeps trying to shut mine down.'

'Then that's the challenge. You'll find a way.'

'I'm sure I picked you to make my life easier.'

'Me too – we're completely compatible. Now I better get out of here before the nurse comes back and throws me out.'

'Thanks for the flowers.' Therese kissed Marian on the cheek and hurried out. Marian lay back down and closed her eyes. *I wish I could remember what happened,* she thought.

Marian went home a few days later, her memory still full of holes and her mind troubled by questions.

Chapter 19

'I think it's time we got you out of here,' Bronte said.

'Yes, I think so, too. I must be almost better; I'm starting to get bored,' Marian said.

'A week's long enough to hang around the house. Come on, let's go.' The sun felt warm on Marian's face, as they walked down towards the ocean.

'Are you alright?' Bronte said, noticing the colour drain from Marian's face.

'I wish I could remember what happened, Bronte.'

'Does it really matter? You got through it and now you're fine.' Marian turned from the waves and stared at the big peace sign across the street. 'Let's go back and see Celia,' Marian said, racing towards the little shop.

The bells tinkled as they opened the shop door. Marian took in her surroundings, realising at once what a good idea this was.

'I'll be with you in a minute,' Celia called from behind the beaded curtain.

'She must be doing a reading,' Bronte said.

'Hmm – I guess so,' Marian said, 'but that little girl shouldn't be out here by herself. Anyone could just grab her.'

Bronte looked around, taking in the dream catchers, the books, crystals and the Buddhas in every shape and size, but they were the only ones in the shop.

'What little girl? There's no-one there, Marian.'

'What's your name?' Marian said, bending down, addressing the empty space in front of her. She nodded, and stood up. 'Come on, let's go and see where your mummy is.'

Bronte froze and watched, fascinated, as Marian stretched out her arm and curled her hand around nothing, then parted the curtain and paused as though she was waiting for someone to enter ahead of her. Bronte hid behind the beads, peering through the small gaps in the long strings, so she could watch the show.

'It's not safe to leave a child wandering around by herself,' Marian said, scowling at the two women on the other side of the curtain.

'What are you talking about, Marian? I'm trying to do a reading for Elizabeth here,' Celia said, an embarrassed flush beginning to colour her face.

'I've brought Eve back to her mother. Do you think it's a good idea to leave your daughter out there in the shop by herself?'

'I don't know what's going on here, but it's not funny,' Elizabeth said, rising from her chair.

'No it's not funny; you should be keeping an eye on her.' Marian turned abruptly and went back through the curtain. Bronte only just managed to escape being hit in the face by the amber beads as they flew in every direction. *She should have been watching her,* Marian thought, the truth dawning on her as Elizabeth entered the front of the shop.

'I only looked away for a second; I'll never forget the noise that car made when it hit her,' Elizabeth said.

'Eve wants you to be happy again. She doesn't want you to be sad. She said she likes the cake you made.'

'It would have been her fifth birthday today. I made her favourite.' Elizabeth left the shop, smiling through her tears. 'You could almost feel the peace settle over her,' Celia said, after she'd seen her out. 'Marian, you have an amazing gift, and I want you to come and work with me, so I may have the opportunity to help you hone it.'

* * *

'Well, I'm glad that's all sorted,' Bronte said, as the two girls walked back to Marian's house. 'I think we just might have that diagnosis.'

'Maybe. Could you really not see Eve?'

'No, but I know you could. And you made her mother so happy.'

'Yes, it must be the most terrible thing to lose a child like that. And to blame yourself.'

'See, you *can* help people, and in the most unique, special way.'

When they arrived back at the house, Marian headed towards her car. 'It's a lot to think about. Let's go for a drive.'

At the sound of the Jeep's engine revving, Sonia tore out the front door. 'Don't you think you should rest? It's only your first time out since your accident.'

'I'll take good care of her, Mrs White. Don't worry,' Bronte said, winding down the window on the passenger side.

They drove along the ocean front and turned sharp left, heading for the city and some retail therapy.

'Do you really think I've lost weight?' Marian said, studying her reflection in the full-length mirror at her favourite boutique. 'This dress looks all wrong.'

Bronte stood back, admiring Marian's svelte figure, wishing she looked half as good.

'You can wear anything. Even a sack would look good on you.'

'Oh, I don't know, but I want to look the part if I'm to start working with Celia.'

Marian took the dress off and pulled the next one off its hanger. As she slipped it over her head, she felt it tighten around her throat.

'I told you I wasn't finished yet,' a voice inside her ear said. Marian struggled to get the dress off, the pressure increasing as she twisted and turned.

'And I told you to leave her alone.'

Marian felt the pressure release from around her neck as the dress finally came up and over her head with ease.

'Got a bit tangled up, did you?' Bronte said, noticing Marian's wild hair and flushed cheeks.

Marian's eyes darted around the changing room trying to remember where she'd heard that voice before. She tried to steady her breathing. *I'm sure I heard Mrs Gardiner too,* she thought.

* * *

Craig tried not to worry but he found himself furiously pacing the driveway, listening for Marian coming around the corner on two wheels. *She drives like a maniac. I can't let her out of my sight.* Marian's accident had taken its toll on him. He'd been questioning his own memory since that awful day and he was in two minds whether or not he should make his own appointment with Dr Maine.

'So how did it go?' Craig said, as Marian's car came to a screeching halt in front of the garage. He opened the driver's door and helped her out.

'I'm fine, Dad. You need to stop worrying.'

'You should tell him,' Bronte whispered. 'Hello, Mr White.'

'Hi, Bronte. Tell me what?' Craig looked from one girl to the other.

It was at that moment that Marian had her first real moment of clarity in a long time. She looked around to make sure her mother was nowhere to be seen, before she opened her mouth.

'I think I might've found myself a career,' Marian said.

Chapter 20

'It's her decision. It's up to her,' Craig said.

'But it's the wrong one,' Sonia said. 'You're *no* help at all.'

'You can't always have your own way, Sonia.'

'What did you say?'

'It's time you opened your eyes – opened your mind to the wonder that is our daughter.'

'Don't be ridiculous. It's because she's so special that I want the best for her.'

'Yes, but only she knows what that is.'

'What are you two talking about?' Marian said, bouncing into the kitchen. Since she'd made the decision to work at Celia's shop, everything made sense. Her mind was open to all possibilities and with Celia's help Marian was going to discover how her talent could really help other people.

'How would you like to help me spend some money?' Craig said to her.

'Why, do you want to buy me something?' Marian said, with a twinkle in her eye as she poured milk on her muesli.

'I thought we could go to the mall and have a look around,' Craig said. 'What do you two think?'

Marian smiled and nodded.

'You two go ahead,' Sonia said, busying herself at the sink. 'I've got a lot to do around here this morning.'

'I'd really like you to come with us,' Marian said. She didn't like her mother being upset.

'And I'd really like you to go to university and make something of yourself,' Sonia said, spinning around, her eyes flashing with anger.

'There's no point in trying to make you understand,' Marian said, a deep sigh escaping her lips as she left the kitchen. She wandered up to her room to change for her outing with her father. As she closed the balcony door, she noticed ominous clouds brewing outside and watched in fascination as they swirled and twisted around on each other. A sudden break revealed a jumble of bright colour, the hues transforming themselves into a vivid scene before her eyes.

Oh, my God, Marian thought, staring up through the glass. The clouds had parted to reveal a crumpled figure – the figure of her mother.

* * *

'Your mother's having a really hard time with all this,' Craig said, putting his seat belt on before starting the car.

'And I'm not?' Marian said, the scene in the clouds burnt into her mind.

'I just want you to be happy. Your mother will come around – you'll see.' *It must be terrible for him – caught in the middle like this,* Marian thought, as she looked out the window at the changing sky.

'I need to see Celia for a minute. Could we go there first?'

'Sure thing – I'd very much like to meet her.'

'She's helping me, Dad. She understands what I'm going through.'

Craig turned the car around and headed back towards the beach. When he stopped at a red light, he noticed the black clouds rolling in over the ocean.

'It looks angry out there,' he said. 'Looks like we're in for a big storm.' He parked the car as close to the peace sign as possible.

That's what I'm afraid of, Marian thought.

'Oh, I like that – very authentic,' Craig said, as the bells tinkled on the door as they entered the shop.

'Me too. Gives the place an old-world charm.'

'I didn't expect to see you today,' Celia said, coming out from behind the counter. 'I hope nothing's wrong?'

'No, everything's fine. I'll be here, bright and early on Monday morning,' Marian said. 'Celia, this is Craig, my father.'

'Very pleased to meet you,' Celia said, smiling and extending her hand.

'Likewise,' Craig said, taking the hand offered to him while admiring her honey-blonde hair and alabaster skin. Her smile dazzled his eyes and tied his tongue.

'I guess you wanted to see where Marian will be working?' Celia said.

'Oh no – I mean y-yes,' Craig stammered.

Marian frowned at her father's awkwardness.

'Can we go in the back for a minute? I need to talk to you about something,' Marian said to Celia.

Celia nodded and parted the amber beads.

'I'll be back in a minute, Dad.'

'It could be a premonition – second sight, or just a plain old flash of intuition,' Celia said after listening to Marian's description of her vision. She wished she could see the world like that. Marian was truly a marvel.

'But she looked all bent and broken.'

Celia bit her bottom lip. 'Intuitive information can sometimes defy logic. The future is dynamic, and although you may sense danger, the universe may only be giving you a warning. Nothing's set in stone. Free will enables us to make choices. Changing your mind can change your future.'

'That sounds like something straight from a book.' Marian couldn't help but smile at the earnest look on Celia's face.

'Well, I must admit, I *did* read it somewhere. And look at you – you changed yours.'

'Ready to go?' Craig said, looking up from the book in his hand, when he heard the clinking of the amber beads.

Celia poked her head through the opening. 'I was just wondering about your mother,' Celia said.

'*My* mother?' Craig said as Marian appeared beside Celia. 'I thought we were here so you could talk about yours, Marian?'

'I guess it's Mother's Day,' Marian said.

They all laughed as Celia led Craig through to the back of the shop.

* * *

'I never realised how hard things were for my mother,' Craig said, shaking his head as he and Marian left the shop.

'What do you mean?'

'A lot of people didn't understand her – didn't accept her. I think your mother's worried things will be the same for you.'

'I have you, and now I know we have Celia. There's nothing to worry about.'

'Except this storm; I think we should head back home.' Craig unlocked the car and slid in behind the wheel.

'Okay, we'll go shopping later.' Thunder rumbled in the distance and lightning danced across the sky. Marian counted the seconds from the bright flash to gauge if the thunder was getting closer.

'So, what do you think of the shop – of Celia?'

'I think you're exactly where you should be.' They pulled up in the driveway just as the first loud crack of thunder echoed across the sky.

'That was close,' Craig said, pulling the garage door down.

'We're home,' Marian called out to the empty house. *Where is she?* she thought, going into the kitchen in search of Sonia and finding it empty. The back door was wide open and the rain was starting to blow in. There was another loud crack and a bright flash of lightning lit up the whole yard.

'That sounds like it almost hit the house,' Craig said, coming into the kitchen. 'Better shut that door.'

'Wait!' Marian screamed, charging out into the wild weather. It was grey night outside now. Freshly washed sheets danced frantically on the clothes line, their stark whiteness contrasting against the dark backdrop.

'Mum, Mum.' Marian's voice was lost in the wind. *She wouldn't leave the washing on the line,* she thought, knowing she was outside somewhere.

'Don't touch the clothesline,' Craig screamed, kneeling over a big crumpled bundle a few feet away.

'Marian – help me get the sheets off the line,' Sonia said, reaching up towards the whiteness.

'Just leave it, Mum. We need to get inside. Come on, Dad.' *What the hell's he doing?* she thought. The rain was so heavy now she could hardly see.

'She's been hit by lightning,' Craig said, running inside, clutching the crumpled bundle to his chest.

'Marian – help me,' Sonia said, clawing at the sheets.

'No – oh no!' Marian cried, tearing after Craig. He laid Sonia's lifeless form on the kitchen table, sobs wracking his body. Marian stood and stared at the broken figure of her mother, wishing with all her heart that this wasn't real.

Chapter 21

'Most people survive a lightning strike,' Dr Emery said. 'It usually zips right over them, but this time it didn't. It gave Sonia an electrical, discharge-induced heart attack.' He was reading from a copy of the autopsy report that Craig had brought with him.

'I just can't believe it. She was here one minute and gone the next,' Craig said, covering his face with his hands and crying softly.

'She should've just left the washing on the line but she couldn't help herself,' Marian said, frowning at Sonia who was hovering in the corner. 'I didn't want Dad to be next so I brought him along so you could have a look at him.'

'Given the circumstances, how are you feeling?' Dr Emery asked Craig.

Craig removed his hands from his face but remained silent.

'Go on – tell him about the chest pain, Dad,' Marian said, annoyed with him too now.

Dr Emery took Craig's vital signs and gave him an ECG.

'Your heart appears to be fine,' Dr Emery said gently.

'Except that it's broken,' Craig said, burying his face back in his hands.

'I'm sure the pain is anxiety related but I'll send you to see a specialist if the symptoms persist. How's your sleeping?'

'He's not,' Marian interrupted. 'Could you give him something?'

Dr Emery nodded, getting his prescription pad out of the drawer in his desk. He wondered at this young woman's strength; she'd just lost her mother and now appeared to be looking after her father. 'And how are you, Marian?'

'I saw a car bumper sticker once that said, *Make sure you live long enough to be a problem to your children.*' She shook her head, a sad smile on her face. 'I thought that was funny at the time.'

'Have you got anyone to help you?'

Marian shrugged and focused her attention towards the corner of the room again. 'She hasn't said anything since she died,' Marian whispered, leaning closer to Dr Emery.

'What do you mean? What're you talking about?'

'Do you remember when I came to see you before and I asked you about your son?'

Dr Emery nodded, his mouth suddenly felt very dry.

'He was the first one I didn't know who appeared to me.'

'Are you hearing this?' Dr Emery said. 'Mr White – Craig?'

'What did you say, Doctor?' Craig's vacant expression became animated for a split second as he looked from Dr Emery to Marian. 'I'm sorry, I was miles away.'

'Well, I need you to try and focus,' Dr Emery said, hoping he was keeping the distress out of his voice.

'She's trying to hold your hand, Dad,' Marian said, fascinated by Sonia's translucent fingers, failing to entwine around Craig's.

'Who – what're you talking about?' Craig looked down at his hands, now resting on the doctor's desk in front of him.

'Mr White, have you got anyone who could come and stay with you – at least until after the funeral?' Dr Emery said. He suddenly felt inadequate to cope with this family's grief; he'd never seen anything like it before.

'I guess I could call my sister-in-law,' Craig said, his wounded expression alarming Dr Emery even further.

'Yes, why don't you do that right now?' Dr Emery said. Craig nodded, reaching into his pocket for his phone.

'No, we'll be fine on our own,' Marian said, dragging her eyes away from her father's hands. 'Mum's still here.'

'Marian,' Doctor Emery said, 'You and your father are going through such a terrible ordeal – you need help – you need family around you.'

'I have all the family I need right here, thank you very much,' Marian said, her eyes darting back towards the corner to where her mother had retreated. 'As do you, Dr Emery,' she said, standing up, ready for the challenge.

'Now, Marian – please settle down. Let's talk about this quietly and calmly.'

'Did you hear that?' Marian said. The two men looked at each other, simultaneously shaking their heads.

'Hear what?' Dr Emery ventured after a moment.

Marian came around to the other side of the big desk and knelt beside the doctor's chair. She spoke to the air beside it. 'What are you giggling at?' she said. 'What've you got there?'

Craig came around the desk to kneel beside his daughter. Dr Emery sat very still. He was too busy deciding whether to call for help or not.

Marian reached for the little boy who was playing with the broken truck – the boy she'd seen here before.

'Mark says to tell you that you're not to worry. He's okay.'

Dr Emery drew in a sharp breath.

'His truck's broken but he can still play with it,' Marian continued.

'I never did get around to fixing it for him,' Dr Emery whispered, the tears streaming down his face. Marian reached up and patted the doctor on the shoulder as she watched Mark climb up onto his father's lap.

'You felt that,' Marian said, seeing the doctor's almost indiscernible flinch as Mark kissed his father goodbye.

Chapter 22

When Craig and Marian got home from Dr Emery's office, Therese was sitting in her car in the driveway. Marian made her way into the house as if she was on a mission, failing to notice Therese at all.

'Thanks for coming,' Craig said, as Therese alighted from her car.

'What happened at the doctors?'

'Come on inside and I'll tell you all about it.'

* * *

'So, Marian said she saw a little boy,' Therese said, when Craig had finished his account of what'd happened.

'Yes, it seems so. She described Dr Emery's dead son – enough to convince him or fool him – I don't know.' They were sitting in the kitchen with the teapot between them.

'And she said that Sonia's still here?'

'Well, you know as well as I do. Sonia always loved being the centre of attention.' They gulped in unison at the use of the past tense.

'Well, we can only deal with one thing at a time,' Therese said. 'It's the only way we'll get through this.'

'The funeral – I need to finish making the arrangements,' Craig said. 'I've got an appointment this afternoon.'

'No, *we* need to do it,' Therese said. 'You don't need to go through this alone.'

'He's not alone,' Marian said, storming into the kitchen.

'Please, honey – let me help,' Therese begged.

'We don't need your help.'

'Why are you suddenly so hostile towards me? Ever since Sonia died, your whole attitude has changed.'

Marian's anger subsided a little as she felt the pain and distress emanating from her aunt. 'I can not only see the dead, I sometimes have a grainy picture of what the future may hold for the living.' Marian looked from Therese to her father. 'But I guess you two won't be able to help yourselves in the end.'

'Stop talking in riddles, Marian. We've got a funeral to plan,' Craig said.

'Yes, the first thing we're going to do is drink our tea,' Marian said, pouring a cup for herself, 'and then we're going to sit here and try to figure out how we're going to help Mum.'

'Your mother's dead, Marian,' Craig said.

'What's that got to do with it?' Marian said to the concerned faces. 'There are two parts to us – our spirit and our physicality. Mum's finished with her body but her soul's still here.' Marian said this to try and help them *all* understand. 'Mum's death was so sudden – she wasn't prepared for it.'

'How do you know this? How *can* you possibly know?' Craig said.

'I know, because they tell me.'

'So, you really did see Mrs Gardiner?'

'I think so. This is all new to me, Dad. I don't have all the answers yet. Some souls wave goodbye and cross over as soon as they die, but some want to stay behind, close to their families for a while.'

'And you believe that's what Sonia's doing?'

'Possibly – she hasn't told me yet.'

Craig stole a sideways glance at Therese, silently pleading for help.

'Can you see her right now?' Therese asked, sweeping the room with her eyes. 'Is she somewhere over there?'

Marian nodded, her heart racing in her chest, as she followed her aunt's pointed finger.

'Am I going insane?' Craig burst out. 'What's with you two?'

'It's alright, Dad. Calm down.'

'Yes, Craig, it's okay.'

'For God's sake! Can we just get this over with?' Craig said.

'I'll go upstairs and pick out an outfit for her,' Therese said, preparing to leave the kitchen. 'Is that okay?'

Craig silently checked with Marian, then nodded his head. He hadn't been able to bring himself to look through Sonia's things. 'Just make sure it's something she'll look good in – something she loved,' he said.

'She looks great in everything,' Marian said. *Even the clothes she's got on now have a touch of glamour,* she thought, noting the bling in the simple dress Sonia was wearing.

'Looked, Marian – looked.'

'I know this is hard to believe. Hell, I hardly believe it myself, but I *can* see her.'

'That may be so, but it doesn't change the fact that she's dead. Now, can we just get on with things?'

'I'll go upstairs and get Sonia's clothes now,' Therese said.

'Okay, then we'll head over to the funeral home,' Craig said. 'First things first, Marian. We can talk about the rest of it later.'

He went out to the car with Marian in tow. Therese appeared a moment later carrying an outfit over her arm.

When Craig opened the passenger side door and offered Therese the front seat Marian said to her aunt, 'No, you sit in the back with me.'

Marian was happy to see her mother sitting in her accustomed place in the front seat next to her father. Craig scowled at Marian but didn't put up an argument. They drove in silence to the funeral home with Sonia's clothes carefully laid between Marian and Therese in the backseat.

'Some spirits remain earthbound and don't cross over at all,' Marian whispered.

'Why would they do that? Is that a good thing?' Therese whispered back.

'There's a few reasons – unfinished business, not believing they're dead, or they're just not ready to go.'

Marian saw Sonia turn around and smile. *She's not ready and neither am I.*

* * *

'Again, please accept my sincere condolences,' Mr Adams said, shaking Craig's hand. 'And thank you for coming and bringing Mrs White's personal belongings. If you'd like to take a seat, we'll prepare her for the viewing.'

They sat in silence, waiting for the unthinkable.

'Are you sure you want to see her?' Craig said, turning towards Therese.

'It's the only way I'll believe it's true,' Therese said. 'I have to see for myself.'

Craig reached over and held her hand. 'I'll be with you,' he said.

'Cut it out, you two – Mum's watching.' Craig released Therese's hand like a guilty man.

'I don't know what to say to you, Marian,' Craig said.

'We're not doing anything wrong,' Therese said.

Oh, but you will be, Marian thought with a clarity that left no question in her mind. 'Shush, here comes the funeral guy,' Marian said, getting to her feet when she saw Mr Adams approach.

'Sonia's ready for you now,' he said in a low, respectful tone.

They followed him to an anteroom. The lighting was muted and there was soft music playing. A white coffin dominated the small space and a few chairs were placed strategically around it.

'I'll leave you to your privacy,' Mr Adams said, backing away from the door.

Craig and Therese hesitated on the threshold but Marian strode boldly in.

Her makeup doesn't look right, she thought, peering over the wooden edge of the white coffin. When she looked up she saw her mother staring down at herself from the other side.

'You were right about everything, Marian.' Sonia choked, reached down and gently touched her own cheek. 'I should've listened to you. I could've known before this.'

Oh my God! She's talking now, Marian thought, as she heard the rusty sound coming from Sonia's throat. 'You had an accident, Mum – these things happen.'

'It's too late now.'

'It's never too late. Death is only another beginning. Everything's on its way to somewhere. Your soul's evolving, getting ready for its next step, that's all.'

'I could've been a better person. What's going to happen to me now?'

'I used to dream of a place beyond the clouds, where peace was the order of the day,' Marian said. 'It was a beautiful place with a magenta sky.'

'You mean, like Heaven?'

'Maybe – maybe you'll go there, when you're ready.'

'Or maybe I'll be dragged in the other direction.'

'Mum, there's good and bad in all of us but you don't have an evil bone in your body.' They fell into silence, gazing down at the body between them.

'Can you fix my makeup?' Sonia said. 'I hate that lipstick on me.'

Marian plucked a tissue from a box nearby, gently wiping off the vermillion, before applying her own pale pink colour to her mother's lips. *They're so cold,* she thought, as she blotted the pink lipstick with another tissue.

'Thank you – that looks much more dignified, considering the situation, don't you think?'

'You always look perfect, Mum.'

'She looks so peaceful,' Therese said, joining Marian by the side of the casket. 'Don't you think so, Craig?'

'They're doing a wonderful job of comforting each other,' Marian whispered to her mother.

'Don't be too hard on them. They'll need each other now,' Sonia said.

'Do you want to send her on with her wedding ring?' Therese said as she admired Craig's family heirloom and not for the first time. 'Maybe Marian should have it?'

'I know who *really* wants it,' Sonia whispered to Marian.

'No,' Marian said too loudly, alarming Mr Adams as he came bustling through the door.

'Are you alright, my dear?' he said, all sympathy and concern.

'Yes, I'm sorry. It was just something my mother said.'

Marian sat in the back seat with Sonia on the way home, nervously twisting the wedding ring around her finger. She stared at her father and aunt sitting in the front, wondering how soon it would be before her father asked for the ring back.

Chapter 23

'I'm sure your mother will go when she's ready, Marian,' Celia said, her voice tinged with concern. They were sitting in the back of the shop, two steaming cups of coffee between them before the day's work began. 'Do you think you may have come back to work a bit early?'

Marian shook her head vigorously. 'I need to be here. It's the only place that makes sense to me right now.' She glanced towards the open window where Sonia was leaning out, deep in conversation with Heston.

Celia reached over and patted Marian's hand.

'You should have seen her at the funeral – just sitting there at the back like any other mourner,' Marian said. 'And you know what she said at the end?' Celia shook her head. 'She said, "Wasn't that a lovely service," as if it had nothing to do with her.'

'I don't know what to tell you. She needs more help than we know how to give her.' They sat there quietly for a few minutes sipping their coffee.

'She just doesn't want to go – that's the problem,' Marian said.

'Is it such a problem?' Celia thought of Heston, just outside the window and yet a million miles away.

'I think she's stuck here but she needs to move on, for her own sake.' *She needs to find her paradise.*

'Marian, I think she's staying here for you. You need to be the one to tell her to go – to make her go.'

'You mean, like you've done with Heston?'

Both women turned their attention to the open window.

'That's different. He's a guardian angel.'

'I remember Mrs Gardiner saying that to me once, in a dream.'

'Are you so sure it was a dream?'

'Well, I haven't seen her lately.' Marian smiled sadly, thinking of her old neighbour. *I hope she's in her paradise,* she thought.

The bell jangled at the shop door. Celia checked the clock above the amber curtain.

'Time to go to work,' she said, taking the empty cup from Marian's hand and placing it on the little sink near the window.

Marian watched Heston reach through the window and gently touch Celia's cheek. A little smile played on Celia's lips as she filled the cups with water. *She doesn't want him to go. She needs him here.* They went through to the front of the shop. There was a sole customer there, turning over an amethyst crystal in her hands.

'This is a lovely piece. I think I'll take it,' the customer said. Celia smiled, took it from her and began to wrap it up.

'Is there anything else I can do for you today?' Celia said.

'Well, as a matter of fact, there may be something you can help me with. I'm trying to organise a get-together – a psychic fair – and I was wondering if you had anyone who would be interested in participating.'

'That sounds very exciting. I went to one a few years ago before I moved here and I've had fleeting thoughts of holding one myself.'

'You mean, here?' The customer took in the small confines of the shop.

'Well yes – there's a ton of room in the back yard.'

'And what a location – so near the ocean. People would flock here once the word was out.'

'So, where were you thinking of holding this event?'

'I was tossing up over a couple of options but it looks as though I may have found the ideal place.'

'I'm Celia, by the way, and this is Marian.'

'Pleased to meet you both, I'm Glimmer. And yes, it's my real name. My mother had a strange sense of humour. Works for me in my professional life though, with readings and such.'

'So, you're a psychic yourself?' Marian said.

'Am I? You tell me, young lady.'

Their eyes locked, and Marian could hear Glimmer's voice in her head. She could see her speaking to a small crowd, dressed in a flowing cape that glistened in the sun while the crowd pressed closer, mesmerised by shards of light shooting from a large, clear crystal she was turning over in her hands.

'That's very impressive,' Marian said, unlocking her eyes from Glimmer's.

'You have to give the people what they want – that's the trick,' Glimmer said.

'Come and have a look at the back room,' Celia said. 'Could you take care of things here for a minute, please Marian?'

'Yes, this'll do nicely,' Glimmer said, going through the beaded curtain ahead of Celia.

'There used to be a door here but I had it removed. I think the beads make a nice touch.'

But Glimmer hardly heard Celia as she looked through the open window into the back yard beyond. 'There's powerful energy here,' she said, leaning through the window and closing her eyes. 'This will make a perfect venue for our big day. This's the right place.' Then she swept back through the curtain into the shop.

Marian tried to stifle a laugh as she watched Glimmer's theatrics. 'She'll pull a big crowd all on her own,' Marian whispered to Celia. 'I wonder if she'll wear that hideous cape.'

'What?' Celia said.

'So, I'll be in touch,' Glimmer said, picking up the amethyst from the counter. 'How much do I owe you for this?' She pulled some money from her handbag but Celia waved it away.

'Please accept it as a small gift. I'm sure you'll put my little shop on the map.'

'Oh, not I – that'll come from another.' Glimmer winked at Marian as she put the amethyst in her bag. She opened the door and flounced out into the afternoon sun, the bells on the door jangling merrily after her.

'Well, she certainly is a character. What'd you think?' Marian said.

'I'm more interested in knowing what *you* think, Marian.'

'You mean about her – about Glimmer?'

'About all of it. What was that thing? That look that passed between you two, for a start.'

'Yes, that was something new. It was like a little story playing in my head.'

'You mean like a vision?'

'I suppose so. All I know is that I can see things inside my head. It's like dreaming when I'm awake.'

'And what about the spirits you see – like my grandfather? How can you tell the difference between the living and the dead?'

'Oh, that's easy. There's a tiny gap between their feet and the ground – so minute you'd hardly notice it. And they're kind of fragile looking, you know? As if they're made of millions of particles that could disperse easily in the wind. But there's nothing fragile about them.'

'They must be amazing to see.'

'I've seen them hold themselves together in fierce winds and raging infernos. They're strong, Celia, tough and determined.'

'I suppose they have to be.'

'What do you mean?'

'I guess death has its side effects.'

The bell jangled on the door admitting three new customers.

'We'd like to be part of your psychic fair, if you have room for us that is,' one said.

'How did you know about the fair? I've barely made up my mind about it,' Celia said.

'Then, what's with the sign?' another said, pointing towards the display window.

Celia ran outside and looked at the notices stuck to the glass. 'Where did that come from?' she said, seeing the new one with its colours that seemed to leap off the page.

'You have to believe in magic you know,' the third said. 'Now, are we in or not?'

Chapter 24

Therese's car was parked in the driveway when Marian got home.

'What's she doing here?' Marian hissed.

'I told you – they need each other now,' Sonia said.

'And you're really okay with it?'

'Well, technically they're doing nothing wrong.'

'Maybe, not yet …'

'Just let it be, Marian.'

Marian put her key in the lock and opened the front door. The smell of home cooking wafted down the hall, assailing her senses with delight and her heart with sadness. *There hasn't been much of this lately,* she thought, thinking of the fast food and the 'no food' she and Craig had been living on.

'How did you get in here?' Marian challenged, walking into the kitchen.

'Surprise,' Therese said, a nervous smile fixed on her face. 'I hope you're hungry.'

'I asked you how you got in here.'

'Your father gave me a key.'

'What! When?'

'The day your mother died. He thought it was a good idea, for safety reasons, you know?'

'Whose safety – yours?'

'I think we should have a little talk,' Therese said, sitting down at the kitchen table.

'Don't sit there – that's Mum's chair.'

Therese jumped up as if the seat was on fire. Marian clenched her hands around the back of her mother's kitchen chair as Sonia sat down.

'Hey, what's going on here, Marian?' Craig said, coming into the kitchen. 'I can hear you all the way out in the driveway.'

'There's nothing much left to do now,' Therese said nodding toward the semi-prepared meal. She picked up her handbag from the kitchen bench. 'You can finish the dinner without me.'

'There's no need for you to go … is there, Marian?' Craig said.

'Sit down, both of you. I want to tell you something,' Marian said, taking the chair next to Sonia.

Therese put her bag back on the bench and turned the oven down.

'Ever since Mum died I've had a funny feeling about you two,' Marian said.

'For God's sake, Marian! This is nonsense,' Craig said, getting up from the table. 'I'm not going to sit and listen to this.'

'I know something's going to happen between you two. It's already started.'

'Is that why you're so angry with me?' Therese said, shaking her head.

'Marian – enough – your mother's hardly cold in the ground and you're speaking like this?' Craig said, throwing himself back down in the chair.

'Mum's sitting next to you, Dad.'

'Well, that's all the more reason for you not to be talking this way, then.' Craig turned to the empty chair beside him, tears filling his eyes. 'I miss her so much.'

'Mum said it's okay – that you two need each other now.' Marian checked with Sonia for confirmation. The sad little smile, the slight nod of the head, almost broke her heart. 'So, I guess I'll try to be okay with it.'

'We all miss her, honey,' Therese said, resisting the urge to throw her arms around the only man she'd ever truly loved.

'You're talking nonsense, Marian,' Craig said, wiping his eyes on the back of his sleeve.

'I'm sorry, Dad. Everything'll be alright – you'll see.'

'No – no it won't. My wife, your mother, your sister is dead. It's *not* alright.'

'Death isn't the end, Dad.'

'Oh, God help me; I can't listen to any more of this,' Craig said, pushing back his chair. He got up and went to check the contents of the oven.

'And as for you, Therese – it's time you stopped denying what you feel,' Marian said.

'What are you talking about now?' Therese said.

'You can't deny you felt Mum's spirit at the funeral home; I could see it in your eyes.'

Therese focused on the vacant chair beside Marian. She resisted the urge to smile. She wanted to thank her big sister.

'That's it,' Craig said, slamming the oven door. 'I don't care if you two can see her – feel her presence – whatever.'

He strode to the back door and went out into the moonlight. He would give anything to see Sonia one more time.

The clothesline creaked in the evening breeze. Craig forced himself to look at the burn mark where the lightning had struck it and he fell to his knees. He reached up to touch the mark of death and he felt a soft, warm hand cover his.

'It will be alright, Craig,' a voice whispered in his ear. 'I'm alright.'

Craig froze, willing the warmth not to leave his hand, not quite believing what was happening and yet what other explanation was there?

'Come inside, Dad. I'm sorry,' Marian said from the doorway.

'Yes, Craig – it's cold out there,' Therese said, standing beside her.

Craig struggled to his feet and went back into the house. 'She's gone, Marian.'

'No she's not. She's sitting in her chair,' Marian said, but the look on her father's face prevented her from turning her head to check. Craig encircled her with his arms.

'She's gone to her rest now – just let her go,' he said. They stood there together, lost in their pain.

'Bye Mum,' Marian said, eventually turning towards the empty chair.

'Goodbye, my love,' Craig whispered, gazing out the back-door into the night.

Chapter 25

'Therese and I were talking last night,' Craig said at breakfast the next morning. 'We were thinking that she could stay here for a while – you know – to help out.'

Marian pushed her plate away. 'Help out how? Help out whom, Dad?'

'I don't like you being here on your own so much, with your mother gone.'

'Well, I wasn't, until you chased her away,' Marian said, then seeing her father's face crumple, 'Oh, I didn't mean that. I'm sorry.'

'We just have to learn to get on with it without her,' Craig said.

'Okay, okay. What scheme did you two concoct while I was sleeping? I guess Therese's been on her own, rattling around in that big, old house for years.'

'Yes, that's right. With her husband dying so young in that terrible accident, as well as having no children, we're the only family she's got. She's hurting as much as we are, Marian.'

I don't know about that, Marian thought, remembering the glint in Therese's eye. 'I suppose I could keep a closer eye on the two of you if she's here. I'll think about it.'

'That's not funny, Marian.'

Marian shrugged her shoulders. 'I've got to get to work.' She left the kitchen without another word.

* * *

Marian was the first to arrive at the shop. She went inside but left the closed sign facing the street. She hurried through to the back room and opened the window, looking for Heston. 'I need to talk to you,' she called. He materialised a second later, looking at her with kindly eyes.

'My mother's gone. I don't know where.'

'No-one's ever really gone, she's just moved. She exists on another plane now,' Heston said.

'I don't care where she is. I just want her back.'

The bell jangled on the door and Celia was there a moment later with two steaming coffees.

'Oh, Marian! What's wrong?' she said, eyeing the back of her assistant's bowed head. 'Here – sit down and tell me.' Celia gently guided her to a chair, offering her a tissue and the coffee.

'Thanks,' Marian said, accepting them both.

'Now, what's this all about?' Celia said, settling into another chair with her own coffee.

'I think Mum's crossed over. I didn't even get to say goodbye.' Fresh tears rolled down Marian's cheeks as she looked around the room for any signs of Sonia. 'I can't see her anymore.'

'But can you feel her in your heart?'

Marian nodded.

'Well then – she's still here.'

'You know, we didn't agree on a lot of things and she was so damn annoying sometimes, but I know she only wanted the best for me.'

'Yes, of course she did. Now, you just need to give yourself some time to let the grief take its course and you'll come out the other side of it with your memories and your love for her intact.'

Marian dabbed at her eyes and looked out the window at Heston who was nodding and smiling. *I know I'll see Mum again,* she thought. 'She must have finished here, I guess. There was no reason for her to stay,' she said.

'That's right; it's time to let her go.'

'You know, she told me I was right about everything.'

'Well, then, you know she'll be okay.'

'I hope so.'

'The best thing you can do is keep busy. It'll help keep you moving forward. Grief has a way of paralysing you if you let it.'

Marian took a deep breath and got to her feet. She threw the empty coffee cups in the bin before she went to turn the sign on the front door around. She met Glimmer waiting at the door.

'I was wondering when you were going to let me in. We've got lots to discuss,' Glimmer said, smiling and kissing Marian on both cheeks.

'And I see you've brought reinforcements with you,' Marian said, noticing a couple standing behind her.

Glimmer's smile disappeared as she turned to look behind her. 'I hope they look friendly! This'll be a special day,' she whispered in Marian's ear as she glided past her into the shop. 'Good morning Celia. I hope I haven't caught you at a bad time.'

'Hello Glimmer. No, not at all. We're just running a bit late this morning, that's all.'

'I've got the final list of interested parties, *finally.'* She waved a piece of paper under Celia's nose.

Celia took the list that was offered to her. 'This many? I thought a handful or two maybe, but this is a very long list,' she said, turning the paper over.

'Let me see,' Marian said, reaching for the list. She scanned the names – one or two of them gave her a bad feeling. 'This looks like a fun bunch but I think there are a couple of questionable entries.'

'Well, it's good to have a mixture,' Glimmer said, waving Marian's concerns away. 'It makes for a much more interesting group.'

'If you say so,' Marian said.

'So, we better get to it,' Celia said, interrupting. She wanted to keep Marian busy so she didn't have time to dwell on her mother's passing. 'What do you have in mind, Glimmer? What's your vision?'

'Oh, this day will be more than spectacular – the best one yet,' Glimmer said, winking at Marian.

* * *

As Marian turned the corner into her street, she saw Therese's car parked in the driveway. *She's here again,* she thought. It'd been a very busy day for her at work with Glimmer rattling on about the psychic fair and more customers through the shop than usual. The smell of baking as she opened the front door assaulted her senses, bringing tears to her eyes again.

'Hello Therese,' Marian said, wiping her eyes with the back of her hand.

Therese watched Marian carefully to assess what sort of mood she was in. 'I'm baking a carrot cake, ' Therese said, flinching, waiting for Marian to order her away from Sonia's domain.

'My favourite,' Marian said, sitting down at the kitchen table. She decided to give her aunt a break. It wasn't her fault she loved her dad. *What's not to love?* she thought.

'I'm so glad,' Therese said, fetching the cake from the oven. 'I finished my article today.'

Marian noticed Therese's open laptop on the far end of the kitchen bench.

'What was this one about?'

'It's called, *A Little Town in Sicily.*'

'It must be nice to work from home – from anywhere.'

'Yes, these days a book review can be done from wherever.'

'Listen, Therese, I know Dad wants you to stay for a while.'

'Would that be such a terrible thing?'

'As I said to Dad – I'll be able to keep an eye on the two of you.'

Therese began to spread the icing on the cake, a slight tremble in her hands. 'I've got a chicken for us for dinner,' she said. 'Now, tell me about your day.'

'Well, we're hosting a fair – a psychic fair – in a few weeks.'

'That sounds interesting. Do you need any help?'

'As a matter of fact, we'll need all the help we can get. It's going to be a huge event by the look of it.' Marian stared at the almost perfect cake, now resting on one of Sonia's favourite plates.

'I could do some baking,' Therese said, following Marian's gaze.

'Yes, that would add a special home-made touch,' Marian said, trying to swallow the lump that had formed in her throat.

'What would add a special touch?' Craig said, entering the kitchen. He noted that the two women seemed to be getting along.

'Hi Dad, I was just telling Therese about the psychic fair we're holding at the shop.'

Craig's brow furrowed as he looked at his daughter. He wondered if she was immersing herself too much in all this psychic stuff. 'Do you really think the shop is the right place for you – especially now?' Craig said.

'Working there's good for me. I'm good at it.'

'I'm not saying you're not but after what's happened …'

'I need to be there, Dad. I want to help people.' *And myself,* Marian thought. Then she told him about Celia and Heston, and about the work she was doing re-connecting this world with the spiritual one.

'So, doing this'll make you happy? This's what you want to do with your life?' Craig said.

'I obviously have this sixth sense, this ability, this insight – call it whatever you like – and I feel I have a responsibility to use it. I want to use it.'

'Then working with Celia could be a good start. Who knows where it'll lead?' Therese said.

'You could become famous. A worldwide sensation,' Craig said. He started to feel a sense of pride for his unique daughter.

Marian blushed but smiled to herself. *Of which one – which world?* 'And by the way, Dad, I think having Therese around for a while would be another good start.'

Therese coughed slightly. She went to the oven on the pretext of checking on the chicken to hide her happy tears.

Chapter 26

'I was wondering if you'd like to come over to my house with me today, Marian,' Therese said.

'I suppose you need to pick up a few things? Don't worry, I meant what I said last night,' Marian said.

'I know you did. You don't work Saturdays, do you?'

'Sometimes, but not this one.'

'I just want to water the garden and check on the place.'

And pack your bags, Marian thought. 'The only thing I want to do today is buy something to wear to the psychic fair. I want to look the part,' Marian said.

'And what part is that – all dark and mysterious?'

'Well, I don't want to shimmer and shake like Glimmer. I was thinking of something soft and flowing.'

'You look good in anything. I always said you should be a model. We can go shopping after we finish at my place, if you like.'

'Actually, I'm meeting Bronte at the mall. I haven't seen her since Mum's funeral.'

'Okay then, we won't be too long.'

* * *

Therese pulled into her driveway and turned the engine off. She looked up at the old family home while Marian was busy answering a text message on her phone. She realised her family were all gone now – she was the only one left.

A tap on the window startled her out of her reverie. Lisa was standing by the driver's window, looking in. 'Are you getting out or are you going to sit there all day?' she said.

Marian dropped the phone back into her bag and opened the car door. 'How are you?' Lisa said, coming around to Marian's side of the car and thinking how sad her friend looked. She hugged her tight.

The three of them went inside and Therese opened the back door. 'It's a bit stuffy. I'll leave the doors open while we're here.'

'We'll go and water the back yard,' Marian said, grabbing Lisa's hand and dragging her through the back door.

'Therese stayed at your place last night?' Lisa said.

'Yes, she wants to help – she wants to be close.'

'Well, I can understand that. Your family's going through such a tragic time, I can only imagine.'

Marian didn't want to think about it anymore. 'Come on – race you,' she said, hurtling towards the lone tree in the middle of the yard. She grabbed hold of the first branch and propelled herself towards the treehouse.

Lisa's eyes widened as she watched Marian cover the distance in a few seconds, an impossible feat.

'I always was faster than you,' Marian yelled, leaning out of the treehouse window.

'Marian – how did you …?' Lisa called back. 'Never mind, I'm coming up. Stay there.'

Lisa grabbed hold of the first branch and the tree shook. A slight vibration passed through her body. She pulled her hand away and took a few steps back so she could look up. The branches were swaying with the slight breeze but that was all she could see. Suddenly there was a loud cracking sound and the tree trunk began to split, rattling the treehouse like dice in a cup.

'Marian – get down!' Lisa screamed, eyes wide with horror.

Therese came running through the backdoor and pulled Lisa away from the base of the tree. 'She's up there.' Lisa pointed a shaking finger towards the treehouse, her voice drowned out by the terrific noise.

The treehouse began to topple. No longer safe and secure, it was ejected from its foundation as the tree expelled it from its old branches.

'Marian, Marian – where are you?' Lisa said, frantically pulling at the twisted pile of smashed timber. Therese raced in to help.

'I'm up here,' Marian answered, but Lisa didn't hear her over the racket she was making in her desperate search for her.

'She's not here,' Lisa said, frowning at the pile of wood. 'I don't understand. Where is she?'

'I'm up here,' Marian repeated, louder this time.

Lisa heard Marian this time but her mind refused to comprehend what she was seeing – Marian seemed to be *standing in the air* next to what was left of the tree. Lisa's head spun and dizziness threatened to overcome her. 'Are you seeing this, Therese?' Lisa couldn't tear her eyes away from the vision above her. 'Have I been hit on the head?'

'See what? What can you see?' Therese said. Therese tilted her head up towards the gnarly ruin. She gasped when she spied Marian's floating form then clapped her hand over her mouth when she noticed the two women hovering beside her. They seemed familiar.

* * *

'Would you like them to remember?' Mina said.

'No, I don't think so, but *I* want to,' Marian said. *Mum was wrong – it's all real – it's not a dream.*

'No, it's not,' Raven said, up to her mind-reading tricks again. Marian stared in awe at Raven floating effortlessly beside her.

Chapter 27

'I should have had that tree taken down with the rest of them,' Therese said, as they surveyed the mess. 'Thank God you weren't hurt.'

'That treehouse meant so much to you – and to me – I know why you tried to save it,' Marian said.

'Well, it's no more now,' Therese said. 'I'll call the arborist to finish the job.'

'You know how they say there comes a point in your life when everything becomes clear; when it's all revealed to you …?' Marian said.

'You mean like an epiphany?'

'Yes, something like that. Well, I think I just had mine.'

Therese didn't know what Marian was talking about but she was more concerned with the near-disaster she now had on her hands.

The side gate opened and Lisa came racing through it, flushed and breathless. There were little scratches on her hands that were starting to bleed. 'Oh, my God!' she said, seeing the mess. 'What happened? Are you both alright?'

'Are *you* alright?' Therese said. 'What happened to your hands?'

'Oh, um, I don't know,' Lisa said, turning her hands back-to-front. 'It doesn't matter …'

'The treehouse decided to throw itself to the ground,' Marian said. 'But we're okay. Come on, let's see about those hands.'

In the bathroom, Marian applied ointment to Lisa's wounds. 'Ouch,' Lisa said when the antiseptic hit.

'It's not too bad – the scratches are only superficial,' Marian said, as she put the first aid kit back under the bathroom sink. 'I'm sorry you hurt your hands.'

'It's not your fault.'

But it is, Marian thought. 'I better go and help Therese,' she said. 'See you later?'

Lisa wandered out the front door, turning her hands over and shaking her head. Marian watched her walk back to her own house and wondered how she would explain those scratches away.

In the back yard, Therese was where she'd left her – surveying the ruins of the treehouse.

'It's a sign to move on,' Marian said softly, squeezing Therese's hand.

'What do you mean?' Therese said, raising her eyebrows.

'You really don't remember, do you?'

'Remember what?'

'Never mind. Let's go home.'

As they got into the car, Marian searched the back seat for Raven. *I was sure she'd be here,* she thought. She knew now, without a doubt, that Raven was back.

Marian headed straight for the balcony of her room when they arrived home, half-expecting one of the chairs to be occupied, but she remained alone. She sat down to ponder what had happened.

The sky began to change colour as the sun went down. Marian watched the colours in the sky change from blue to a beautiful magenta. She drew a sharp breath and flung herself towards the balcony railing. She forgot to breathe; she forgot everything in this world as she lifted herself from it and propelled herself up to the one above.

It was the same as she remembered it in her dreams. *But they weren't dreams – it really did exist.* The great expanse of magenta water came into view as Marian alighted on the soft ground beside the water, close to the people milling around it. One turned, and then another until Marian was confronted by a sea of smiling faces. Panic threatened to engulf her as she stood there – exposed – a stranger in a familiar place.

She nearly jumped out of her skin when she felt a light tap on her shoulder. 'Henry,' Marian said, spinning around, 'you're here.' Her heart missed a beat at the sight of him.

'Where else would I be?' Henry said. 'I've been waiting for you.'

'As have we all,' another voice said from Marian's dreams.

'Imogen – oh, Imogen,' Marian said, sinking to her knees. 'It's real. It's all real.'

'Yes, my dear – welcome back.'

'Yes, you finally made it all on your own,' Margot said, helping Marian to her feet. 'Congratulations.'

'Margot! I can't believe it.'

'Believe it, Marian. It's really here.'

'But what are you doing here? Aren't you with your husband?'

'Oh, he's happy where he is. He's fine and I'll certainly join him later down the track, but for now, I'm here for you, for real.' She looked at Marian with the same kind eyes that had sparkled with mischief when she was alive. 'You'll do wondrous things here … and there,' Margot said, casting her eyes downwards.

'Yes, and I'll help you too,' Raven said, pushing her way through the crowd. 'Just as I always have.' There was no way she was going to let the old lady upstage her.

WHEN THERE'S NO-ONE THERE

'We're all here to support you, to help you grow into who you will become,' Mina said, appearing at Raven's side.

'You're famous up here, you know,' Raven said. '*Everyone* wants to meet you.' She narrowed her eyes as she thought about her real home, wishing she was there now.

'I don't think I'm so special,' Marian said, a blush turning her cheeks a deep red. 'Nothing compared to all of you. This is just like a spectacular homecoming.'

'Your sweet nature and your humility are two of your shining attributes,' Imogen said. 'Now, I think we need to talk. Please excuse us, everyone.'

Imogen led Marian away from the crowd, over to a small glass table surrounded by huge cushions. As they sat, the table top began to swirl and shift until a sharp picture came into focus.

'It's not exactly a crystal ball but the principle's the same,' Imogen said, concentrating on what was being revealed.

'Who's that?' Marian said, seeing a face looking back through the table.

'Oh, that's not important right now. We've more pressing matters to discuss. I knew you'd be back when you were ready. I can see the change in you – the certainty – a developing maturity. I've been watching your progress with great interest and I'm amazed at what you've achieved on your own. The way you conducted yourself when your mother passed was extraordinary.'

'How is she? Where is she?' Marian turned her head, half-expecting to see her materialise.

'Sonia's settled and happy in her paradise and you'll see her when you go to yours.'

'So, she's not here?'

'As I've explained before, this is a final stop on the journey – a place to be sure all is finished and done in the land of the living, before the paradise begins. You'll be an invaluable asset – you'll be able to bridge the gap.'

Imogen reached out her hand and stroked Marian's cheek. 'You're extraordinary. The first living soul to ever enter The Magenta Sky before death – a true miracle.'

'So, Mum had no unfinished business then?'

'That lightning strike opened her eyes. She stopped being afraid. All she needed to do was make sure the three people she loved most in the world were going to be okay, then she left.'

Marian let out a deep sigh and pondered on what Imogen said. 'Well, if I can be sure of re-uniting with her, then I guess I'll be alright.'

'That's the spirit. And this may help – look.' Imogen pointed to the image on the table as it began to shift and change again. As its new revelation came into focus, Marian was almost blinded by the pure white light. 'She's there – safe with the pure souls.'

Marian felt such a peace come over her – such a feeling of certainty – that all her doubts were dispelled in the warmth and the clarity of paradise.

'I've been thinking a great deal about your return and what it means,' Imogen said as the white light began to dim.

'You know, at first I thought I was losing my mind.' Marian said. 'When I saw Mrs Gardiner – Margot – after she died, it felt as though a part of me woke up.'

'That was a very powerful moment for you – very confronting.'

'Then when Raven came back, I really began to fear for my sanity.'

'What's this – did I hear my name mentioned?' Raven said. She'd been skulking behind a nearby tree. 'What are you two talking about?'

'We were having a private discussion, Raven,' Imogen said.

'You can't keep her all to yourself – we're all anxious to spend time with her.'

'I know you're not the most patient of souls, Raven, but I would like a moment alone with Marian, if you please.'

'Not going to happen – look.'

The crowd had inched closer and now threatened to press itself around the three women.

'There's no harm in everyone being here, is there?' Marian said, bathed in the glow of the love surrounding her.

'I was only trying to explain …' Imogen said.

'Then tell us all,' Mina said, pushing her way through the throng.

'Alright then,' Imogen said, settling back to begin her story, as the crowd gathered at her feet.

Raven laid a possessive hand on Marian's shoulder, hoping that Imogen would tell the short version. She tried to look interested but she'd heard it all before – from Gregory. He was her counterpart in The Grey Dusk, her real home, and he'd sent her here to this awful place full of light and love.

As she listened to Imogen drone on, she thought about how difficult her mission had been – to secure Marian for the deep and dark. It had been so long in coming to fruition. *All I want to do is get Marian away from here – get her safe and sound below,* she thought.

Imogen's voice broke into her thoughts. 'So, you see, the energy now resides in Marian. She can come and go between us and the living.'

And she can just keep on going, Raven thought, wishing she could get Marian out of there. *Oh, the power we'll have, when we get her over to our side. Such an injustice, that Imogen discovered Marian before we did.*

Chapter 28

The fire beckoned as it came into Raven's view. *This's the light I love,* she thought, as she zeroed in on Gregory. He was in his usual place before the cold, raging inferno.

'So, the girl has finally figured it out. And about time. That treehouse falling – inspired work,' Gregory said, as Raven alighted beside him.

'I had nothing to do with that. That was just a happy coincidence.'

'Hmm – maybe, but no matter. It finally woke her up to herself. You won't be missed?'

'They're all so preoccupied up there with the coming of their little goddess they won't notice that I'm gone.'

'Jealous?' Gregory raised an eyebrow, knowing full well she was.

'Of what? Of Marian? Don't be ridiculous.'

'You really have done an outstanding job. Getting close to Imogen the way you did and then being assigned to watch over Marian – you've fooled them all.'

'Maybe, but it's not over yet. I still have to get her here.'

'And you will. You will complete your mission.'

They fell silent, their gazes drawn to the flames. Gregory conjured the scene up above. He stared at Imogen with hungry eyes while Raven coveted Marian.

'Look at the way she is with that Henry,' Raven said. 'She's supposed to be helping him – directing him to his damn paradise – but I think she really wants to keep him for herself.'

Gregory dragged his attention away from Imogen to observe the other interaction that was taking place. 'Hmm, this could be our phase two – our new strategy.'

'A new strategy?'

'Well it's obvious. Can't you see? Marian's ripe for love – she's dying to fall in love.' Gregory turned from the fire, searching his flock.

'What about him?' Gregory pointed to a man hovering on the edge of the shadows.

Raven waited for the man to turn around in response to Gregory's silent summons. As he slowly swivelled his head, Raven watched the firelight play on the perfect features of his face.

'I can see I'm on the right track,' Gregory said, observing Raven's reaction.

'What? Did you say something?' Raven said, barely able to tear her eyes away from the new arrival.

'Never mind – you'd better be getting back.' Gregory turned back to focus on Imogen in the fire.

'I will soon. But first, can you tell me the story? Tell me again how this's supposed to go.'

'You have a very special purpose,' Gregory said, as Raven settled back, ready to listen to this story he'd told her many times before. 'You were chosen for a reason because you have that spark of goodness in you, the spark that protects you and lets you go undetected anywhere – everywhere.'

Raven nodded, fighting the impulse to run to the perfect stranger she'd seen at the edge of the crowd.

Gregory recognised her struggle and delighted in it, envisioning Marian also falling under his spell.

'Good and evil are two sides of the same coin, existing together,' Gregory continued. 'Every soul has a measure of both until the deciding day; the day when it either wants paradise or to be dissolved into blackness. Following Imogen's discovery of the recipient of the energy, you were strategically placed in her way, playing the part of the lost soul, to gain her trust. Your aim was to become as close to Marian as possible, to become indispensable in her life. You'll bring her here when the time is right and we'll discover what she can really do.'

'But I'll have to make her want to come. She must come with me willingly or she won't make it past the gate.'

'Yes, that's the rule that must never be broken. But don't despair. Love is a powerful energy. It too can stand alone and we'll make it work in our favour. Do you feel better now?'

'I just want this to be over.'

'Then get back up there and let me think.'

* * *

Gregory watched Raven ascend before he sauntered over to speak to the newcomer. All eyes were upon him as he parted the crowd. They were fearful of him; he could send any one of them careening into an eternal blackness on a whim.

'Welcome – welcome to The Grey Dusk,' Gregory said, extending his hand. 'And you are?'

'Jasper Hope.' The man eyed Gregory with suspicion before accepting the hand that was offered to him.

'I trust your death wasn't too unpleasant, Mr Hope.'

'My death ... is *that* what this is?' Jasper appreciated his surroundings with a new perspective.

'And what terrible atrocity have you committed?'

'I don't see how that's any of your business.'

'No matter, let me explain how things work down here.' Gregory knew full well why Jasper was there. He knew why they were all there and he knew The Blackness awaited them all when the time came.

'So, you enjoyed your way of life?' Gregory said.

'It was good while it lasted.'

'How would you like to go back – continue where you left off?'

'I thought there would be no escape from Hell.'

'There's no way out of The Blackness, but you're not quite there yet.'

'So, I could go back?'

'Perhaps.' *I need a second chance,* Gregory thought, staring into the fire, his own past laid out before him. The glint of the sun as it reflected off his executioner's axe caused a familiar thrill. He watched, as it came down hard and precise. He could still feel the weight of it in his hands, like an extension of his body. Relieving the guilty of their heads had been his job. The act of killing wasn't his crime but the way he lived for killing had been. The sin stemmed from the rapture he felt as each head rolled away.

'What's it like – you know – in the next place?' Jasper said.

'Tormented peace – endless – all-consuming.'

'How do you know, if you've never been there?'

'I'm the exception. I've been as far as the gate. I've gazed through those bars into the never-ending night. I was summoned to receive my orders from the Ones in The Blackness before I was assigned here. I make the decisions. I decide when time's up.'

'And what's the purpose of *this* place – this Grey Dusk?'

'There's no defined point where "light" stops and "darkness" begins. They both exist on a graduated continuum. It's the same with people. Each of us has a balance of negative and positive or nasty and nice, and by the time we die, we're either on a path to endarkenment or one of enlightenment. The Blackness is one extreme of the spectrum – there's no coming back.'

'Then, I have a chance of redemption?'

'Slim, at best, considering your crimes. Very clever the way you lured in those poor, trusting fools then delivered them to evil.'

'Being a psychic had its merits and its thrills. The dark side appealed to me more, I suppose.'

'You enabled more than one of my flock to feel the earth beneath their feet again.'

Jasper smiled, thinking of the large payment he had received for his services from the living. He remembered how they never saw it coming and the swift, decisive action of each possession.

'You may cross paths with some of them again,' Gregory said, rubbing his hands together. 'In the meantime, I have a job for you. I need you to get in someone's way – to steal a heart.'

'Oh, you mean Marian? Consider it done.' Jasper peered into the fire, conjuring her face. 'This fire's like a window. How interesting. This death thing doesn't seem to have robbed me of my ability. It may even have been enhanced.'

'Maybe so.' *He could be more useful than I anticipated,* Gregory thought, resisting the urge to rub his hands together again.

Chapter 29

'Raven, where have you been? I've been looking for you every-where,' Imogen said. 'It's imperative that you stay by Marian's side.'

'Of course I will. We finally have her back. Can you believe it?' Raven said, clapping her hands while thinking that the nightmare was nearly over.

'We must be on our guard now, more than ever. We must be vigilant. There are others who know of her existence.'

'I don't understand – what others?' Raven's eyes narrowed. *What does she know?* she thought.

'There was a man here once – a confused, beautiful soul. I was his angel and he was my greatest challenge.' Imogen's eyes misted over as she remembered Gregory. 'I watched over him in life and guided him here after death.'

'Where is he now? What happened to him?'

'I sent him away. He gave me no other choice but to banish him.'

'Because he wasn't perfect?'

'Because he let the dark side of his nature quash his glorious light.' Imogen remembered how much she'd tried to get Gregory to change, how she'd pleaded with him to embrace the light, but the dark had the stronger pull on him. 'We are all but a combination of the light and the dark but one is always dominant – there's always a winner in the end,' Imogen said, looking deep into Raven's eyes. She hoped she wasn't going to lose another one. She couldn't lose Raven too.

'And these others? What do you know about them?' Raven said.

'They want Marian for their own ends. To be on their side. They reside in The Blackness.'

'And what about this man you sent away, where does he fit into the scheme of things?'

Imogen hesitated. This would be a huge revelation for Raven and she didn't want her careening off into the dark again. 'He's their leader now – the leader of The Grey Dusk.'

'So, he was here – with you?' *That's not possible – that can't be true,* Raven thought.

'As I said before, we are light and dark but a side must be chosen before we can move on. We all have a choice.' Imogen's penetrating stare cut through the barricades Raven had erected around her heart. She'd decided Raven wasn't all bad but wondered if she'd done the right thing taking a chance on her.

'And what choice do you think Marian will make?' Raven said, raising an eyebrow. 'How good do you think she really is?'

'What're you talking about? Marian has a pure heart.'

'But how do you know for sure?'

* * *

After Raven had gone, Imogen wandered over to her glass table. *She has a point,* she thought, staring into its swirling top. As she waited for the image to clear, Imogen wondered what she really knew at all.

She reminisced about the time she first held the reins of The Magenta Sky, when she'd stood on the threshold of her paradise, with its endless white serenity. The gates of light had beckoned but Imogen felt the pull of unfinished business preventing her from making her entrance. The Pure Souls had explained things carefully to her, turning her around and charging her with her special purpose.

How can I keep all the lost souls safe? she thought, staring into the table. The image sharpened to reveal a wild-eyed Raven, hands on hips, throwing an accusatory glare at a laughing Gregory.

'Why didn't you tell me?' Raven screamed at him.

'Calm down! I can explain,' Gregory said, trying to stifle his laughter.

'Oh, this'll be good.'

'It wouldn't have made any difference if you had known about my past. And I didn't want you distracted by it.'

'Distracted by it? You still should have told me.'

'Raven, you were sent to The Magenta Sky to get close to Marian, not to wonder about Imogen and myself.'

'I don't care. I just can't imagine you as one of them.'

'I never was. That's why I was thrown out. I was given a chance to change but I didn't want to. I liked how I was – how I am. The Ones in The Blackness were impressed by my resistance. They thought I had what it takes to be here – to have control. I have the power to make *all* their decisions.'

'I think we're all very well aware that we work for you.'

'Not for me – for the greater good.'

'A poor choice of words, don't you think?'

'Good, bad, it all depends on the point of view – whose side we're on.'

'Well, which side are we on?'

'Our side – the right one. All we need now is Marian. She can stop the waste – direct the souls here, away from any paradise and swell the ranks, increasing the power of The Blackness, so it can obliterate all light.'

'So, did you love her?'

'Who, Marian? What are you talking about?'

'Imogen, Gregory – did you love her?'

'I'm not capable of that kind of love. I'm a narcissistic bastard. You should know that by now. You should return before you're missed. I have work to do.'

'Can I help?'

'You already have. Jasper!'

Jasper obeyed Gregory's summons at once. 'So, I hear you're the genius who gave Gregory this fine idea?' he said to Raven. He looked her up and down and watched her squirm.

She couldn't meet the appraising look in his eyes. She didn't trust herself. She realised she could never let anyone else have him, especially Marian. 'I don't know whether it's an idea we should seriously consider,' Raven said, forcing herself to meet the penetration of Jasper's stare at last.

'Nonsense! It's a stupendous plan and Jasper's the perfect choice to execute it,' Gregory said, enjoying Raven's discomfort. He imagined that Marian would move Heaven and Earth to be with him.

'Excuse me,' Raven said, 'I have things to attend to.'

The two men watched after her flustered figure as it was swallowed up in the gloom.

'I've never known her to be lost for words before. I think our plan will work,' Gregory said.

'Then I'd better get started.'

Chapter 30

'Marian, are you listening to me?' Celia said.

'Oh, sorry, I was miles away,' Marian said, dragging her attention back to Celia and Glimmer.

'Is there anything you want to tell us? You seem somewhat distracted,' Glimmer said, peering into Marian's eyes, but unable to detect any clues to her behaviour.

'I'm just going through some stuff. I'll figure it out,' Marian said. She could see Raven hovering in the corner of the shop.

'Is it anything to do with Therese and your dad?' Celia said.

'What? No, no! Mum gave them her blessing. She was okay with it, so why shouldn't I be?'

'Then what is it?' Glimmer said.

'I've seen a whole other world that I'm a part of,' Marian whispered.

'Well, of course you are. We all are,' Celia said.

'Tell us about this world,' Glimmer said, noticing how Marian kept glancing towards the corner of the room.

'I have the ability to travel there.'

'Like astral travel?'

'No, like *real* travel, 'Marian said, and then she gently levitated a little off the ground. Celia and Glimmer stared in revered silence, unable to move – unable to think – as they watched the miracle before them.

'Who else knows about this?' Glimmer said, the first to recover enough to speak. Her eyes darted around the room, searching for any hidden danger.

'No-one, except those up there,' Marian said, pointing sky-wards. *And those down there,* she thought, not wishing to alarm her two companions any further.

'Let's keep it that way, alright?' Glimmer said. 'Celia?'

'I don't believe this,' Celia said in a small voice, shaking her head. She was mesmerised by the small space between Marian's feet and the ground.

'They'll all want her,' Glimmer said, taking a protective step towards Marian.

'Well, they'll have to get through us first,' Celia said, taking a protective step of her own.

'We may be able to garrison protection from our own psychic community. Thank God we're holding this psychic fair,' Glimmer said.

'This must have been the reason you appeared in the shop that day,' Celia said to Glimmer, remembering the first time Glimmer filled the shop with her unique flamboyance.

'Everything happens for a reason,' Marian said, floating up to touch the ceiling.

Celia and Glimmer stood transfixed by the sight before them; tears flowing freely from their barely believing eyes.

'We must keep this between us for now,' Glimmer said, pulling herself together. 'Marian, come down and tell us all about it.'

Marian gently walked down through the air until her feet touched the floor.

'Oh, my angel,' Celia said, folding Marian in her arms.

'No, at least not yet,' Marian said, her eyes drawn towards the corner once again.

'What do you keep looking at?' Glimmer said.

'Raven – my angel. We began our journey together when I was a little girl. She was the imaginary friend of my childhood who turned out to be my very real guardian angel.'

'What does she look like?' Glimmer said, furiously searching for pencil and paper. 'Another one of my many talents is spirit drawing, although I usually rely on the vision that presents itself inside my head. Could you describe her for me please?'

'You mean like a police sketch artist, or something?' Marian said.

Glimmer nodded – her pencil poised, then she went to work as Marian described what Raven looked like.

'Oh, she's lovely. We should frame that,' Celia said, leaning over Glimmer's shoulder.

'Yes, that's her,' Marian said as Glimmer held up her finished work. 'What do you think, Raven?' Marian took the sketch over to the empty corner and held it up for Raven to see. Of course, to the other two, it looked as though she was showing it to thin air.

'Let me have it back a minute, please Marian,' Glimmer said, reaching for the paper. She looked closely at the pencil strokes, at the eyes that seemed to bore a hole right through her. 'They know Marian's here,' Glimmer said, dropping the sketch on the floor at Celia's feet.

Chapter 31

'We'll need to act fast. I think they're onto me,' Raven said, her eyes searching The Grey Dusk for Jasper. 'Where is he?'

'Don't you worry about a thing. Our plan's already been executed,' Gregory said. 'It was only a matter of time before you aroused suspicion. But don't worry, Marian will always defend you, no matter what.'

'Even if she finds out the truth about me?'

'Especially if she finds out; she'll want to save you. You need to understand that it's her compassion and her sense of what's right that'll be her downfall.'

'I don't understand – what do you mean?'

'Marian will take on all the troubles of all the worlds. Once we get her down here and let her see the suffering and the pain, she'll be ours. We'll manipulate her mind; we'll rally our own crusade until she bends to our will. And that, my dear, is where Jasper comes in. If he can win her heart, we'll win her.'

'Love conquers all, you mean?'

'Something like that.' Gregory turned towards his leaping flames. *If Marian comes, so will she,* he thought, imagining what he would say to Imogen when he finally had the chance. 'Jasper's with Marian now.'

'No, he's not. I've only just left her.'

'Jasper has a unique ability that makes him ideal for this mission. He can hide himself or reveal himself – appear alive or dead, depending on the situation.'

'What? Now you're confusing me.'

'He can stay by Marian's side and watch her – learn her ways – understand what makes her tick and make his move at the right moment.'

'So, he's with her now?'

Gregory nodded, stifling a laugh. *She's definitely jealous,* he thought.

'I think I'll go and see if there's anything I can do to help,' Raven said, making ready to leave.

'Yes, you do that, but remember our plan. And don't you go falling for him yourself.' His laughter finally escaped as Gregory threw back his head and let it out. *This's going to be most entertaining,* he thought.

* * *

Damn Gregory. And Marian can go to Hell. I don't need any of them, Raven thought. She appeared in a corner of the shop, finding Marian serving behind the counter. Glimmer was beside her while Jasper stood directly behind, almost pressing himself up against her body. *And damn you too, Jasper.* Raven threw him a scathing look. He caught the look and slid over to her corner.

'Marian can't see you. She seems totally unaware that you're even here,' Raven said.

'Yes, I'm deliberately keeping myself hidden from her. I've placed a cloak of secrecy around myself.'

'Something like their white light of protection?'

'Ah, yes, but it's so much more.' Jasper closed his eyes and became very still. His body glowed with life as he planted his feet firmly on the wooden floor.

'How did you do that?' Raven said, marvelling at the sound of his boots clicking on the floor.

But Jasper paid her no attention. His sights were on Marian as he walked deliberately out of the corner and stood directly in front of her.

'I'm sorry, I didn't hear you come in,' Marian said, looking up from the appointment book.

'I can see that you're engrossed in your work,' Jasper said, sidling up to the counter.

'Um, may I help you?'

'Well, let's see … what have you got to offer?'

Marian felt a heat spread across her cheeks as this strange man looked her up and down.

'Perhaps I could let you discover my secrets?' Jasper said, inclining his head towards the amber curtain.

'Is that what you want?'

Their eyes locked in a silent challenge, Jasper congratulating himself on his duplicity and Marian wondering why a dead man seemed so desperate to appear alive.

'Is everything alright, Marian?' Celia said, parting the curtain. 'Does the gentleman require a reading?'

'Unfortunately, I have a prior engagement. Good day, ladies.'

'We're holding a psychic fair here next weekend,' Marian said. She hurried from behind the counter and pointed to the sign in the window. Dead or alive, she wasn't ready to let him go just yet.

As he reached the front door, Jasper paused to cast his eyes over the notice. 'Yes, that could be most entertaining,' Jasper said, before disappearing out into the street.

'You need to stay away from him. He's trouble, Marian,' Raven said, watching the look of longing on Marian's face as she focused on Jasper's retreating form.

'What do you know about it?' Marian craned her neck to catch the last glimpse of Jasper before she turned on Raven.

'I don't know anything.'

Marian saw the look of longing reflected in Raven's eyes. 'You're lying. You're not telling me the truth.'

'You don't know what you're talking about.'

'Don't I? Who sent him? My side or yours?'

Chapter 32

Marian opened the front door and looked around the house. It was like she was seeing it all for the first time. Therese had been making subtle changes since her sister died and now there was barely any trace of Sonia left.

'You've always loved him, haven't you?' Marian said, finding Therese where she always was – in the kitchen. Therese spun around, losing control of the wooden spoon she had in her hand. Tiny splatters of sauce flicked up onto the splashback above the stove.

'I suppose there's no point in denying it,' Therese said, placing the spoon carefully in the sink. 'But I accepted long ago that he chose Sonia.'

'And now it's your turn?'

'I'll make him happy, Marian, I promise.'

'I hope so; he's been through so much.'

'We all have, honey.'

Marian sat down at the table. *It is good having her here,* she thought. 'There's something else I want to talk to you about.'

Therese sat down at the kitchen table wondering what she was going to hear now.

'I want you to tell me about Mina.'

'Not that again. I thought we'd finished with all that.'

'I want you to renew your friendship. I want you to accept what you're capable of.'

'Marian, that was a long time ago. I have more important things to occupy my mind with than retreating into a fantasy world.'

'Is that what you think I'm doing?'

'Honey, I don't deny that your intuition is off the radar and I don't deny that I can sense things, but I don't want any part of it.'

'Any part of what?' Craig said, entering the room, dropping a kiss on the top of Marian's head and another on Therese's cheek.

'I was just asking Therese if she could help me with something at work next weekend.'

'Oh yes, the psychic fair. Is there anything I can do?' Craig said, planting himself in a chair.

'Apart from picking up the extra tables and chairs, I think we're fine thanks, Dad.'

'What will Therese be doing?' Craig said.

'I just want her to be there.'

'Of course, we'll both be there – won't we, Sonia?' Craig said. His smile froze on his lips as he realised he'd called Therese by her sister's name.

Therese gulped and her face flamed red. She vowed silently that she would never again come second best.

'So, you'll come then, Therese?' Marian said, appearing oblivious to her aunt's discomfort.

Therese took a deep breath. 'Yes, and I'll think about what you said about Mina.'

'Mina?' Craig said.

'Never you mind, Craig. She's just an old friend.'

'Okay, then – that's settled,' Marian said, rising from the table. 'I've got stuff to do.' She left the kitchen, closing the door quietly behind her.

* * *

'It just slipped out. I'm sorry Therese,' Craig said, as the door clicked shut.

'That's okay – just a slip of the tongue,' Therese said, stirring so hard, drops of sauce joined what was already splattered on the splashback.

'You know there's always been a place for you in my heart.'

'Bad timing then?'

Craig shrugged his shoulders and stood up. He prized the spoon from Therese's hand and put it down.

'I think Sonia always knew. She just wouldn't take no for an answer.'

'Yes, she always had to get her own way.' Therese remembered the day she took Craig home to meet her sister and how Sonia had stolen him away. 'I won't be second best. I've been there my whole life.'

'Just give me a chance to show you how special you are,' Craig said, folding her in his arms. Therese melted into the warmth of Craig's embrace. *I've waited so long for this,* she thought, as she closed her eyes and breathed him in.

Chapter 33

'The dead need to be heard just as much as the living. They have just as much to say,' Marian said.

'And probably just as many questions,' Celia said.

'Especially those who were ripped away suddenly,' Glimmer said.

And there are more than enough of them here, Marian thought, standing in the open area behind the shop, keeping a track on the arrivals. They were coming through the side gate and raining down from the sky. 'We'll have to be on guard for any possibility,' Marian whispered, looking pointedly down at the ground.

'Absolutely,' Glimmer said. 'Dark spirits or shadow ghosts, negative and troublesome, attach themselves to the living, sometimes by accident or for fun, or just so they can continue to experience life.'

'They can be helped to move past the temporary prison their minds have created with counselling, advice and understanding,' Celia said. 'Just like a psychologist, a psychic can convince them to move on – to go on to the better things that await them and to help them understand that although their bodies have died, their souls still live, and they only need turn towards the light to find their freedom.'

Marian applauded. 'Yeah, stuff like that. That sounds like an opening speech.' She couldn't resist smiling at the two women.

'Well, I have prepared a little something,' Celia said.

'And I've sent more than my fair share of confused souls in the right direction,' Glimmer said.

'Well, we make a great team, then,' Marian said, linking arms with them both. 'Let's see what this day brings.'

'Then, I declare this psychic fair open,' Celia said.

'Yay!' Glimmer said, disappearing into the crowd, her robe catching the sun, sending little sparkles into the air.

'She certainly looks the part,' Therese said, coming to join them. 'Craig dropped me off. He said to call him if we need anything. You must be Celia.'

'It's so good to meet you, Therese. Marian's told me so much about you.' Celia thought Therese looked nice; not like a home-wrecker at all.

'Yes, likewise. I'll go and man the coffee machine, shall I?'

'Yes, thank you so much for coming to help,' Celia said.

'I'm nervous about meeting all the others,' Marian said to Celia after Therese had left. 'I don't have anywhere near the experience they have.' Her eyes roamed around the crowd.

'Ah, but you have raw talent – a gift none of us could ever hope for. Now, come on, let's mingle.' Celia weaved her way through the crowd, introducing Marian around, showing her off. 'There are so many people here and it's all because of you.' She joined a group of people a short distance away, leaving Marian to her own devices.

What a crowd, Marian thought, distracted by the light reflecting off the crystal balls, the impossibly colourful robes, and the rhythmic sound of chanting. *I wonder if he'll come. I don't even know his name.*

'It's Jasper,' a voice whispered in her ear.

Marian spun around, almost losing her balance. Jasper placed strong hands on her, preventing her from toppling over. 'You gave me such a fright,' Marian said, taking a step back.

'I'm sorry,' Jasper said.

'I don't think you are.'

'You're beginning to figure me out already,' Jasper said.

'So, *Jasper* – what are you doing here?'

'I came to see the show.'

'No, I mean here – here with the living.'

Jasper's smile vanished along with his tenacity when he realised she knew he was dead. 'Oh, the usual – unfinished business and all that.' He plastered the smile back on his face but his confidence was shattered.

'Maybe I can help you?'

'I hope so. My business is with you.'

'With me? I don't understand. I don't even know you.'

'Oh, but we all know who you are.'

Marian felt a knot forming in the pit of her stomach. 'We?'

'Well, you already know Raven.'

Raven, who'd been watching the interaction with Marian and Jasper closely, couldn't hold her tongue any longer. 'Leave her alone, Jasper, and don't drag me into this. Don't listen to him, Marian. He's just a troublemaker.'

'You know each other?' Marian looked from one to the other in surprise.

Raven hung her head but Jasper threw his back and laughed again. 'You could say that,' he said.

The knot in Marian's stomach tightened as reality came crashing in. 'Raven, you can't be one of them; I would have known.' Her eyes were wide with horror, her fears confirmed.

'You don't know how hard it's been pretending to be your friend; pretending to care,' Raven said, all pretence now vanished. 'Thank God that's all over now.'

'God? So you can't be thoroughly evil.'

'Oh, you think you're just so clever, don't you?'

'And what about Imogen and Mina. You fooled them too?'

'Those two are just so busy finding the good in people, they can't see what's really going on.'

'And what *is* going on, Raven?'

'I think I can answer that,' Jasper said, interrupting. 'We come from a much darker place than you can ever imagine – ruled by a tyrant – Lord Gregory. We have no choice but to obey him or he'll plunge us into eternal blackness.'

'That sounds like the script from a bad movie,' Marian said, watching Raven's face.

'It's true! He made me do it,' Raven said.

'There are many others down there under Lord Gregory's control,' Jasper said.

'That may be so, but you all must have done something to be sent there in the first place. Get out of my sight, the two of you.' Marian dismissed them with a wave of her hand and turned away. There was no way she was going to give them the satisfaction of seeing her in tears. She wiped them away with the back of her hand.

* * *

Glimmer had watched Marian gesturing wildly to the space around her. 'Celia,' she called. 'Something's wrong with Marian.' She hurried over to see if she could help. 'Everything okay?' The pain she saw reflected in Marian's eyes told her things definitely were not. 'Here, come and sit down.'

But Marian didn't seem to hear her. 'I need to speak to Imogen about this,' Marian said, her feet beginning to leave the ground.

At that moment, Therese looked up from the coffee machine just in time to see the tiny slit of light begin to appear between

Marian's feet and the ground. Her mind blasted wide open as she finally accepted the truth she could no longer deny.

'I don't think that's a good idea,' a voice said softly in Marian's ear. She turned her head to face cold eyes of stone. 'We don't want everyone to know your little secret now, do we?'

Marian could feel herself falling into those eyes like a black abyss with no end. A cold pressure wrapped itself around her wrist, holding her prisoner. She shook her head to break the power of his gaze. 'Let go of me. Leave me alone,' Marian said, struggling to escape, as the grip on her wrist continued to tighten.

Therese flew to Marian's side. 'Let her go.' She forced herself between Marian and the man who held her in his vice-like grip.

'I need no interference from you,' the man said, taking his attention off Marian for a second and riveting his cold eyes on Therese. Then he saw an opportunity. Therese had fallen under his spell straightaway. He released his grip on Marian and smiled at them both. 'I'm so sorry, Marian. I was only trying to protect you – to keep you safe. I'm Lamar and I am at your service.'

'You can *see* him?' Marian said, turning incredulous eyes on Therese.

'Oh yes,' Therese said breathlessly, barely able to tear her eyes away from the most beautiful man she'd ever seen.

'You can really see him?' Marian said again. 'I can't believe it – after all this time …'

But Therese barely heard her as she stood stock still, mesmerised by the man's eyes. Lamar winked at her and bowed before fading into the crowd.

'Come back,' Therese said, her voice laced with desperation as she raced after Lamar's disappearing shape.

'Marian, what's wrong? What's happening?' Glimmer said, confused by the unfolding events.

'I'm not completely sure but I think Therese can see ... I have to find her.'

Glimmer watched Marian tear off through the crowd in pursuit of Therese. She began to follow but tripped as she became entangled in her cape. She threw it off with a dramatic flourish and followed Marian as fast as she could, but she lost her amidst the hustle and bustle of the fair.

'Did you see where she went?' Glimmer said, almost running into Celia who had also given chase.

'She's gone that way.' Celia raised her eyes to the sky.

'Oh God! Did anyone see her?'

'No, she went out through the shop. I tried to catch up with her but she was too quick for me.'

'And what about Therese?'

'That stupid woman's wandering around in a daze looking for some dead guy.'

Chapter 34

Therese opened the car door and stepped onto the concrete drive-way. It was good to feel something solid beneath her unsteady legs. Her whole body felt so weak, she had to hold onto the car for a moment. She didn't think her legs would carry her the short distance to the house.

'Where have you been?' Craig said, opening the front door and peering out into the darkness. In the dim light, he could just make out Therese's silhouette leaning on the car. 'I've been worried. It's getting late.'

Craig turned the front light on and gasped at the stricken look on Therese's face. 'Are you alright?' Craig said, flying down the front steps.

Therese could hear his voice but it sounded a long way away. She opened her mouth to answer him, but nothing came out. Her fevered mind was filled with only one thing – the man she had met at the fair. The moment she had laid eyes on Lamar, all else had left her mind. Her thoughts were stripped of everything but him.

'Come inside,' Craig said, placing a protective arm around her shoulder, leading her towards the front door. 'Where's Marian?'

Therese looked at him blankly and wandered into the kitchen.

Wondering what was wrong with her, Craig followed closely behind. 'Therese, where's Marian?' He thought something must have happened at the fair. Images of mass hypnosis played like a movie through his frantic mind.

Therese continued to stare straight ahead as the minutes ticked by.

'This is ridiculous, I'm going down there,' Craig said. 'Come on, I can't leave you here in this state.' He grabbed Therese's hand and began to pull her down the hallway. Just as he was about to lock the front door, the deafening screech of brakes caused the keys to slip from his trembling fingers. 'Thank God, she's home,' Craig said, steering Therese back inside the house.

'I've been looking for her everywhere,' Marian said, when she saw Therese's car in the driveway.

Craig watched Marian bound up the front steps, relieved she was okay. 'There's something wrong with her, Marian.'

'Yes, I know. I think she's in shock.'

'What do you mean? God, ever since Margot died we seem to limp from one disaster to another. We've had more death, more disturbances in our lives in this short time, than most families have in their entire lifetimes.'

'I think I'll go and have a bath,' Therese said, finding her voice at last. She walked slowly from the room, giving neither Craig nor Marian a backward glance.

'She looks like she's seen a ghost or something,' Craig said, shaking his head.

'Or something,' Marian muttered. She could still feel traces of the cold pressure on her wrist.

'What? What did you say?'

'Dad, I think Therese can see … you know, like I can.'

Craig felt the room spin a little as he struggled to comprehend what Marian was trying to tell him.

'And Dad, I think I'm in trouble.'

The forlorn expression in his daughter's eyes sent a wave of panic through Craig. He stopped feeling sorry for himself and tried to pull himself together. 'What kind of trouble?'

'I think I've had this all wrong.'

'Here, come and sit down. Tell me what's wrong,' Craig said, pulling out a chair for her.

'No, no – I'll show you,' Marian said. She stood very still for a moment, then she slowly began to rise. She hovered a few feet above the kitchen floor, the tears streaming down her face. 'I never asked for this, Dad.'

Craig watched his daughter ascend, his ties with reality shredded to bits. 'My God, Marian! What've they done to you?' Springing into action, he grabbed Marian's legs and anchored her to him. He pulled her down until her feet were firmly back on the kitchen floor. Craig held his daughter close as he finally accepted what he already knew deep down. He remembered that catastrophic day down at the beach when Marian had almost drowned; how he thought she'd been dead but had come back to him somehow. He let go of her and stared, incredulous at the wonder that was his daughter.

'Sit down and tell me everything,' Craig said. 'And please don't float away again. I don't think I could take anymore right now.'

* * *

Therese sat on the edge of the bath, staring into the running water. *I need to find him – I need to see him – I need him,* she thought. Her infected mind didn't notice the water spill over the edge of the bath and onto the tiled floor.

'I think the bath is full enough,' Lamar said, his face forming through the steam. 'Turn the taps off, my love.'

Therese reached out with shaking hands to stem the flow, her eyes never leaving his as she submerged into the steaming water.

Lamar was disappointed that his conquest was so easy. His instructions from Gregory had been very clear: he had to get Therese to enter The Grey Dusk.

Newly dead, Lamar was nowhere near ready to go careening into The Blackness. His life on earth had been cut short by a jealous husband's bullet. He loved the ladies – the chase, the challenge and the ultimate conquest. This task was hardly worth his while but if it kept him from a blackness he wasn't yet ready for …

Jasper's failure had been revealed to both Gregory and Lamar as they looked into the cold fire. 'Never send a boy to do a man's job,' Lamar said.

'I think we can get to Marian through her aunt,' Gregory told him. 'Therese is vulnerable at her core, while Marian has an impenetrable strength and a real intuition. I need to get her here.'

A slow smile spread across Lamar's face. 'Leave it to me.'

Lamar snapped back to the present. He turned to the woman in the bath. 'Now, my dear, let me help you relax.' He applied pressure to Therese's shoulders with his hands – gentle at first – then stronger, coaxing her body under the water. She began to yield, letting the water cover her chin and then her entire face.

'Not like that,' Raven whispered in his ear. 'If you kill her, she'll ascend. She'll be out of our reach.'

Lamar jerked away from Therese and looked down at her. He saw the longing in her eyes mixed with confusion, as he backed away.

'Enjoy your bath, my love,' Lamar said, before evaporating with the steam.

'I don't understand all these damn rules,' Lamar said, joining Raven in the gloom. They travelled in silence back to the cold fire and the furious look in Gregory's eyes.

'You very nearly ruined everything,' Gregory said, raising his fist in the air. Raven waited for the bolt of lightning that would signal Lamar's imminent destruction. 'But I saw a hunger in Therese's eyes – a craving for you. This still might work,' Gregory said.

'What do I need to do?' Lamar said. He hadn't taken his eyes off Gregory's raised fist. He watched in relief as Gregory relaxed.

'Lamar's no good to us,' Raven said, observing the lowering of Gregory's fist with a keen disappointment.

'Be quiet, Raven,' Gregory said, his fist beginning to rise again, 'or you'll be next.'

'What – me – after all I've done for you?'

'Get out of my sight before I change my mind,' Gregory said, dismissing her with a wave of his unclenched hand. He watched her retreat before turning his attention back to Lamar.

'You just need to remember that Therese is innocent. Your assignment is to make her guilty,' Gregory said.

'I'll see to it that Therese can't live without me. Thank you, Gregory.'

'I don't want your thanks. Just get her here.' Gregory waved Lamar away before turning brooding eyes back towards the fire.

Chapter 35

'I can't believe Raven's one of them,' Marian said, pacing up and down beside the magenta lake. 'It can't be true!' She fell to her knees, her body wracked with sobs, the pain of betrayal beginning to rip through her, as though her heart had been scored by a sharp knife. Marian couldn't even begin to accept Raven's duplicity. 'I should have seen *something.*' Marian rocked herself back and forth on her knees, trying to accept the truth about the little friend who had been so much a part of her life. 'I won't accept it.'

'She was perfect in her disguise,' Imogen said, kneeling beside the distraught Marian. 'You certainly weren't the only one to be taken in by her false demeanour. I knew what she was and I failed to save her.'

'What are you saying? You knew she was bad?'

'I had hoped to give her the second chance she needs but I ran out of time.' Imogen's beautiful face was marred with sadness as she thought of the little cherub who had once tugged at her heart strings and had now severed them forever. 'I'm not fit for my position here. I belong down there with her.'

'Don't be so ridiculous. Stop blaming yourself,' Mina said, kneeling on the ground beside them.

'But I'm the one to blame. I'm responsible for the safety of The Magenta Sky.'

'Now you listen to me,' Mina said. 'The Pure Souls would never have given you this position of trust if they didn't have absolute faith in you and in your judgement.'

'This isn't the first time,' Imogen whispered. 'There was Gregory…'

'Gregory?' Marian said, her mind snapping to attention.

'Raven was never ours to begin with,' Imogen said. 'If only I hadn't been so naive.'

'The only thing you're guilty of – if anything – is seeing the light in us all,' Mina said.

'This isn't getting us anywhere. How are we going to save Raven?' Marian said, casting an imploring look over Imogen and Mina.

'We aren't, my dear. She's chosen her own path,' Imogen said gently.

'But it's the wrong one,' Marian said.

'Maybe not for her,' Mina said.

'You told me once that there's good and evil in us all. I believe it's just the level and depth that varies. I'll get Raven back.'

The determined look in Marian's eyes left no room for argument. She looked so sure of herself – so determined that Imogen almost smiled.

'My dear, that's exactly what they want. They want you there.'

'And who was this other failure of yours, this Gregory?' Marian needed to know that Imogen's man wasn't the same one who was now controlling Raven and Jasper.

'Yes, it's true. I failed him. Now he languishes in a place of no return.'

'The Grey Dusk? You sent him to The Grey Dusk?' Marian said.

'You know of it?'

'Yes, Raven has told me about her home and I know who's in charge down there.'

'I'm sorry, I've failed you too, Marian.'

'Don't you see? If Gregory was accepted here once, he can be again. Everyone deserves a second chance and I see now what it is that I'm supposed to do. I'm to give it to them!'

Imogen began to weep a mixture of sorrow and joy as she realised the truth of Marian's words.

'You deserve a second chance too, Imogen. I'll get both Raven and Gregory back for you.'

During her descent, she thought of the other poor lost souls languishing in a grey place. *They must still have a little hope or they wouldn't be there,* she reasoned to herself. Then Jasper's face appeared in her mind and she felt the fluttering of butterflies in her stomach. *His second chance is with me.*

* * *

'Is Therese still in the bath?' Marian said, as she appeared in the kitchen. Craig lifted his head from his hands and glanced at the clock.

'It hasn't been all that long. Did you find what you were looking for upstairs?'

Marian struggled to remember the excuse she had given her father for leaving the room. The clock in the kitchen had virtually stood still while Marian had been realising her true purpose. She was excited and humbled to know that she was about to embark on her life's work of saving the dead.

'I might as well tell you all of it,' Marian said, taking a seat at the table. 'There's a place beyond the sky…'

Craig sat as silent as stone as he let Marian's revelations sink in. It was all too fantastic to be real but he'd seen her levitate not once, but twice now with his own eyes. The rest, this Magenta

Sky, this Grey Dusk, were but extensions of the impossible. His mother made him a believer long ago and now his daughter had confirmed the wonders of the spiritual world for him. But what Marian could do was far beyond rational thought. Belief and faith were the tools needed for this and Craig was ready to throw caution to the wind and embrace it all with a steadfast conviction.

'I guess that's why you chose me to be your father,' Craig said when Marian paused for breath.

'I hope you don't mind too much.' Marian reached out to touch his hand.

'You're more than gifted – more than special.' Craig grabbed her hand fiercely with both of his. 'You have the power to change the world.'

'I just want to help people. As a doctor, I could save the living but this way I can save the dead.'

'Whatever you need … whatever you want from me…'

'I know, Dad. Thank you.'

'And Sonia's really okay?'

'Yes, I promise you. And I can guarantee you'll see her again.'

Craig sat back in the chair, a serene expression replacing the troubled lines on his face.

'Thank you – thank you for picking me.'

'I think I'll go up and see what's keeping Therese,' Marian said.

Craig glanced at the clock again. He'd almost forgotten about her. 'Yes, I want to know what happened to her today.'

'I just want to see if she's alright. Maybe the three of us can talk?'

This will be my first real test, Marian thought. She touched her wrist where the cold pressure had been. As she climbed the stairs, she thought about how Raven had left her clues, but she'd chosen not to see them.

The bathroom door was open but the room was empty. Marian continued down the hall looking for Therese.

'Therese, where are you?' Marian asked the empty rooms. Then she heard a little laugh. Marian followed its tinkle and found Therese lounging in one of the chairs on the balcony of her room.

'What are you doing in my room?' Marian said, 'and what are you laughing at?' Marian checked the small space but Therese was alone.

'Oh Marian, what a glorious day!' Therese said, looking up at her with shining eyes.

Craig appeared at the opening of the sliding door. 'You've come back to life! What are you doing out here?'

Therese shrugged her shoulders and remained silent.

'Therese, what's going on? I know there was someone here,' Marian said. *And she thought she knew who it was too.*

Therese said nothing. She stood up and walked away from them, the bland expression returning to her face.

'Not so fast,' Marian said, grabbing hold of her arm. 'We need to talk about what happened today – about what you saw.'

'You're the one who sees things, Marian – not me,' Therese said. Their eyes locked together in a silent challenge as one acknowledged the truth and the other denied it.

Chapter 36

'So, how's Therese? Is she on the mend?' Glimmer said.

'I don't know what's wrong with her. She hasn't left the house for three days now – ever since the fair,' Marian said.

'I think she's hiding.' Celia joined them carrying a tray holding three steaming coffees.

'Thank you, we've certainly earned this,' Glimmer said, accepting her mug.

'Yes, the shop's never been so busy,' Celia said, turning the sign over in the window and locking the door. 'The fair was a resounding success.'

'Except for what it's done to Therese,' Marian said.

'Like I said, she's hiding,' Celia said.

Glimmer nodded, her lips forming a thin line. 'She's in denial. She's hiding from the truth.'

'No, no there's more to it than that,' Marian said. 'I know she saw that dark spirit – Lamar his name was.'

'The shock of seeing you begin to lift yourself off the ground opened her eyes,' Glimmer said. 'And I think she saw him because he revealed himself. He wanted to be seen.'

Marian shivered as she remembered those cold eyes as they bored right through her. 'Now I'm positive he has Therese in his sights,' she said. 'He's appearing to her. He's trying to take control of her.'

'This'll have something to do with you, mark my words,' Glimmer said. 'An attempt to capture you, perhaps?'

'You're scaring me, Glimmer,' Marian said.

'You have nothing to fear – right is on your side.'

'Yes, but does right always win?' Marian imagined Raven cheering for the bad guys.

'We shall gather all our resources,' Glimmer said, fetching a pad and pen from the shop counter. 'We'll call a meeting of the higher minds and talk strategy. There will be no need to reveal the extent of your abilities. We'll form the circle and conjure the protection.'

'The higher minds?' Celia asked.

'My devoted followers. They'll do anything for me and now they'll be there for Marian.'

Marian wandered over to the big window that made up the far wall and peered out. The sky was alive with dramatic colour set against the sunset gloom. 'I want to know what Heston thinks,' Marian said.

'Celia's grandfather will be of immense help,' Glimmer said, scribbling on her pad. 'Is he here?'

'He's never far away. I just wish I could see him,' Celia said, pressing her face up against the glass.

Marian opened the window as the old soldier materialised out of the gloom, the last of the day's light glinting on the medals on his chest.

'You're about to be tested,' Heston told her, a serious look replacing the usual sunny smile on his kind, old face. 'The three realms are now aware of your existence.'

'Three?' Marian said.

'Now that Celia, Glimmer, Craig and Therese share the privilege of your greatness, the knowing is complete.'

'So, what am I supposed to do – save all the worlds?' Marian said. She sighed, thinking of the mammoth task ahead.

'My dear girl, you are the beginning of all possibility. You're the one we've all been waiting for. No-one will harm you. You're worth too much to us all.' Heston retreated with the last light of the day but his silhouette remained standing to attention.

Marian glanced at the astounded faces of Glimmer and Celia. *I can trust them,* she thought as her feet left the floor.

Celia gasped and dug her fingers into Glimmer's arm. 'I still can't believe it,' Celia said, unable to tear her eyes away from the sight of Marian standing in the air. 'Are you a spirit, Marian?'

'She is and she isn't,' Glimmer said. 'Her spirit is free before her death. It's as though she's missed a step.'

'Or gained one,' Celia said.

'You really are a wonder. I will protect you with my life,' Glimmer said. Marian lowered herself back down to the floor. 'Let's hope it never comes to that.'

Chapter 37

'Where's Therese?' Marian said, coming in through the back door of her house. She felt a little better after her talk with Heston. She'd left Celia to lock up and Glimmer to consult with her higher minds. She smiled to herself as she realised she really did have the best people in her corner.

'In the bath,' Craig said.

'Again! I thought she hated baths.'

'She says they make her feel better.' Craig shrugged his shoulders and opened the fridge door.

'She needs to accept the truth about herself. That'll make her feel better.'

'And what *is* that exactly?'

Marian shook her head. She didn't want to alarm him by telling him about Lamar. 'I can't get her to talk to me. All I really know is that she has some ability to *see*.'

'Do you think Mina was real? You know, her childhood friend?'

'You know about her?'

Craig nodded. 'Your mother told me.'

'She never could keep a secret.' They shared a sad smile and felt the living memory between them. Craig let out a deep sigh and went back to rummaging through the fridge. 'What do you feel like for dinner?'

Marian peered over his shoulder into the almost empty recess. 'There's not much to choose from. How about take-away?'

Craig shrugged his shoulders again. 'Sounds good to me,' he said, retrieving his car keys from the kitchen bench.

Marian thought he looked like he carried the weight of the world on his shoulders and it unnerved her. Anger began to boil deep down inside her as she thought of her aunt languishing in luxury upstairs. *Therese needs to get her act together and treat Dad better than this,* Marian thought. She clenched her fists and headed to the bathroom.

'Therese, we need to talk!' Marian said, banging on the door. 'Could you please get out of that damn bath? I'll wait for you in my room.'

While she waited, Marian leant on her balcony railing and looked up, hoping for inspiration. *I don't know what I'm supposed to do but I know I possess the ability to do it.* When many minutes had passed and still no Therese, Marian marched back to the bathroom door with renewed determination.

'Therese, are you alright?' Marian pressed her ear to the door. But there was only silence. 'Therese! Can you hear me?' Marian turned the door handle and encountered an unfamiliar resistance.

Panic began to take hold making Marian's chest tight. The bathroom door was never locked. She tore down to the kitchen, reaching into the junk drawer for the spare set of house keys. She ran back to the bathroom fumbling for the right one. *Come on, come on,* she prayed, as her shaking fingers failed to grasp the bathroom key. Suddenly, the right key was in her hand and she had the door open. *Where is she?* She peered over the edge of the shining white porcelain tub. Therese's body lay on the bottom, under the water, still and lifeless.

Marian shrieked. 'Oh, my God!' She tried to pull Therese's head up and out of the cold water, but it was too heavy. She searched frantically for the plug wedged under the body, and managed to pull it out. As soon as the water was shallow enough, she jumped into the bath on top of her, clamped her mouth around Therese's blue lips and tried to breathe the life back into her. She compressed her chest, willing Therese's heart to beat again but her life refused to be coaxed back.

Marian heaved herself off the body and out of the bath. She staggered back to the bathroom door, and closed it to try and contain the horror. Then she lay on the floor in a crumpled mess, unable to move, beaten and broken.

'She's chasing a ghost,' a voice whispered in her ear.

'What?' Marian said, the sound echoing in the dead silence. She sat bolt upright, searching for the source. 'Jasper?' she said, searching his eyes for answers as he knelt beside her.

'She's gone after Lamar.'

'But that means …'

'Yes, she's gone to The Grey Dusk.'

'But she's not a bad person.'

'No, but she's committed a crime that's sent her there.'

Marian jumped to her feet, fear and anger propelling her into action.

'I have to get her back. She didn't mean it. He made her do it.'

'No, Marian. Lamar was very careful not to. If he'd taken her, she would have ascended. It was her own choice.'

'She wanted him that much she killed herself?'

'Her judgement was clouded by desire; a desire she obviously couldn't control.'

'I don't believe that for a second. She waited so long to be with my father. Lamar did *something* to her.'

'Nothing she didn't want.'

'She'd never do anything like this on her own.'

'Marian, I've seen her. She's down there with Lord Gregory.'

Marian stole a look over the edge of the bath. Therese looked anything but peaceful, her face displaying a desperate expression in death.

Jasper waited for Marian to accept what had happened, visualising his triumphant return to The Grey Dusk with Marian by his side.

'How can I help? What can I do?' Marian turned away from the bath and looked Jasper directly in the eye. There were no butterflies now, just a gnawing need for help. 'Are you on my side? Can I trust you?'

'Of course I am. You know you can.' Jasper held Marian's gaze, his lies disguised, he hoped, by her need for him.

'Then, take me there,' Marian said.

Jasper grabbed Marian's hand, raced along the hallway to her balcony and pushed her over the railing.

'Are you trying to kill me too?' Marian said, righting herself and standing in the air.

'Now what good would that do me?'

'What do you mean by that?'

'Nothing – nothing, just wait …'

The air rippled below her floating feet as a whirlpool began to appear. It was deep and dark and Marian could feel she was on the threshold of Hell. There were no pretty colours, no smiling faces, just a menacing swirl of air spinning and yawning beneath her feet.

'The universe is but a series of doors which we all must pass through on our way to enlightenment or endarkenment. We can choose until we reach the final door.'

'You mean Heaven or Hell?'

'The reality is that things are rarely as simple as that. We all retain our free will long after death.'

'So, Therese could come back?'

Jasper shook his head. 'Not as she was.'

'But look what I can do.'

'Yes, you're this amazing exception, and none of us know what to expect.'

'Are you being sarcastic?' Marian stared at the spirit she was about to trust with her life, knowing she didn't have a choice.

Jasper shook his head. He could almost taste the glory that would be his when he delivered the precious Marian into The Grey Dusk.

Marian braved a look at the expanding, swirling space below her. It looked as though it went on forever. She stretched her legs towards it, closer to its brink and felt it grip and take hold of her. *I wonder if I'll ever see the light of day again,* she thought, as she let it suck her down into the unknown.

Chapter 38

The whirlpool wrapped Marian in a cold cocoon as it pulled her down into its murky swirl. She could just make out Jasper's form beside her through the dim light. She looked down through the vortex as a grey glow began to appear.

Marian had a vision of terrifying fire and brimstone and as she came closer, she could see the glow from pockets of fires scattered about the dull landscape. There was one roaring inferno with grey shadows huddled around it, and it was there that the swirl released her, spitting her out on the grey, dusty ground.

Gregory was staring into the flames – into his orange crystal ball. He had seen Marian coming before she'd left the safety of her balcony. He was elated beyond words to see his plan coming together and he was in awe of this young girl who had such incredible power. Never in the history of The Grey Dusk had a living soul entered. Gregory absently wondered if she would be cold or if the air would seem stale to her. He had ceased to breathe so long ago now.

Raven was standing beside him watching Marian descend. 'She must have conjured that whirlpool up herself somehow. I didn't know such a thing existed,' Raven said.

'She's wonderful! Amazing!' Gregory said, pressing his hands together in a parody of thankful prayer. 'And now she's mine.'

'What're you going to do with her? You're not going to hurt her, are you?'

'You needn't concern yourself with Marian anymore and I don't want you here when she arrives.'

'I *knew* you'd say that,' Raven said, moving away and melting into the shadows. Raven realised she *had* to go; she wasn't ready to face Marian. Cheering and dancing in the firelight didn't seem appropriate somehow. *I miss her. She's the only real friend I've ever had,* she thought, grimacing at Gregory who gave her a final dismissive wave before turning his back on her.

Gregory's full attention was now riveted on the figures coming closer. As the distance shortened between them, Gregory felt his confidence ebb. It was all so hard to believe. His nerves began to fray.

'Lord Gregory,' Marian said, cautiously approaching the fire. 'I'm sure you know who I am and why I've come.' She scanned the sparse landscape for Therese but Marian couldn't pick her out from all the other sad, huddled creatures.

Gregory bowed in the presence of this incredible girl. 'Lady Marian – welcome.'

'Marian will do just fine. Now, where is she?'

'The new arrivals are in quarantine,' Jasper said.

'Silence! I need no help from you,' Gregory said. 'You are not permitted to speak.'

'You leave him alone,' Marian said with a sudden ferocity. 'I don't know what Jasper did to deserve the pleasure of *your* company but he's a good man.'

Jasper's mouth fell open at Marian's words. He was unable to meet her eyes.

The smile vanished from Gregory's face in an instant. He realised that he had no idea what he was up against or what would happen next. He'd been focused for so long on this moment, he'd never contemplated the next step. He'd expected a little hesitancy from Marian, maybe even a touch of fear, but he could detect nothing even remotely like that in Marian's manner. Nobody, dead or alive, knew what this girl could do – least of all her, but here she was, ready to do battle.

'Tell me, Marian – how's Imogen?' Gregory said, desperate to throw her off balance.

'Imogen? *My* Imogen?' Marian said.

'Yes, we're old friends.'

'She was here?' Marian searched the area, trying to imagine Imogen as a part of the grey. 'Or did you know her when you lived?'

'Ah, no … we met after.'

'You mean, you were *there?*' Marian thrust her index finger skywards.

Gregory nodded his head, his composure evaporating.

'Is that what this is all about?' Raven said, appearing from the shadows. She stood before Gregory, her eyes burning with anger. 'You lied to me. You used me. All this was so you could get Imogen here?'

'That's only a part of it. The Ones in The Blackness want Marian. They want her here for their own means.'

'And I thought you were incapable of love. Yet all this time …' Raven said.

'And who are they? The Ones in The Blackness,' Marian said, ignoring Raven's outburst.

'The Ones in The Blackness run the show. We all have to answer to them,' Gregory said.

'Not me. I don't answer to anyone,' Marian said. 'Now, where is she?' She squinted into the gloom surrounding them but it was too hard to see anything clearly.

'We all answer to someone, Marian, and you'll answer to them if you ever want to see Therese again,' Gregory said.

'And you'll answer to me if you don't give her back,' Marian said. She placed her hands on her hips and scowled at this dead man who stood between her and saving her aunt. Anger began to burn its way through her body as she waited for him to make his move. He took a step toward her then suddenly backed away. Gregory's face was alive with light. It seemed to ricochet off him and back to her. Marian stared at her hands. Light, like a million stars, shot from her body and out into the gloom. She threw the light into every corner of The Grey Dusk – an illuminating, warming light such as this grey place had never seen. Sad souls turned away from the cold fire and reached out to a warmth that had been lost to them. Some shunned it, afraid. They ran screaming into The Blackness, deciding for themselves that their time had finally run out.

It was then that Gregory could see who Marian really was. She was the light. She was the hope. She gave a choice back to the ones who *had* no choice. The Grey Dusk was unrecognisable to him. It was now made up of black and white. He gazed in awe at this girl who seemed to be made of light itself and who penetrated the dark.

Gregory had no defence against her. Her light almost blinded him and its warmth burnt through to his dark soul. He didn't know how to handle this situation. He needed fresh orders.

So he went out beyond the fire, beyond the hope, and out into The Blackness. He followed the screaming horde hurtling itself away from the bright light, escaping it like it was a leaking poison. He went deeper into The Blackness, down to where the ones that ruled dwelled. He feared their wrath; he'd deserted his post. Marian was where they wanted her but Gregory knew that would earn him little mercy.

Marian's light shone on the poor faces of the souls who remained, bathing them in the first thing they'd felt since being sent to this unholy holding bay. Pandemonium erupted as they reached for her. Pale and pathetic, they clambered over each other and on top of one another, desperately trying to capture her warmth. Marian attempted to propel herself out of harm's way, to levitate herself out of danger but her body was anchored to the dust. The crowd threatened to suffocate her with their frantic demands. She retreated a step backward to make some room between her and them but encountered a large rock. She scrambled up it to try and escape the inevitable crush and to continue to search for Therese.

'You need to get out of here. Let me help you,' Raven said, appearing by her side.

Marian looked down from the temporary safety of her vantage point to the seething horde below. She could see that Raven was right. They'd suck the light right out of her if they could reach her.

But Marian couldn't trust Raven. 'Go to Hell!' She spat the words at Raven who let out a hollow laugh.

'Are you serious? Look around you.'

Marian didn't have to look; she could feel the depth of despair suffocating her like a heavy cloak. *This place could be a taste of Hell – the end before the end,* she thought. She looked down at the wretched souls caught here in this grey place, unable to move on, unable to decide their own fate. *So many to save.* She searched again for the only one she was interested in right now, but Therese remained invisible.

'Raven's right, we need to get you out of here,' Jasper said, grabbing hold of her arm.

'Not without Therese,' Marian said, wrenching her arm free.

'We'll come back for her,' Jasper said.

'We don't even know if she *can* leave,' Marian said. 'I can't bring her back to life, can I?'

'After what I've just witnessed, anything's possible.'

'And where's Lord Gregory? I need him to let me take her.'

'He's gone … and he's no lord. He's run away like the lukewarm leader that he is,' Lamar said, ejecting himself from the crowd.

'You! What did you do with Therese?' Marian said, her eyes ablaze with fury.

'Nothing she didn't want, my dear,' Lamar said. 'Now, I suggest you get out of here and let me get on with running this place as it should be.'

'Gregory will be back,' Raven said, casting her eyes towards The Blackness, willing him to emerge from its inky depths. 'You're in no position to make any decisions.'

'Are you going to challenge me?' Lamar said.

Raven hung her head in the face of Lamar's conviction.

'I thought not,' he said. 'The snivelling coward may return or The Blackness might swallow him forever. But he's gone for now.'

'I need to see Therese,' Marian said. Her light began to fade as despair invaded her heart. The crowd began to disperse along with the light as the sense of hopelessness returned.

'It will do you no good. Therese is mine now,' Lamar said.

'We'll just see about that. Where is she?' Marian could feel the anger begin to burn again.

Lamar stepped aside to reveal a crumpled figure. It looked like a statue with its wooden stillness. A cloak shrouded its features as it stood silent and bent. Lamar whipped the covering off with a flourish to reveal a barely recognisable Therese.

'Oh my God, what've you done to her?' Marian said. She was as pale as the ghost she'd become – her eyes dead and lifeless. Marian could see those eyes held no recognition as she searched Therese's face.

'Death has been most unkind to her but I have every confidence that I can restore her to her former glory,' Lamar said, prodding the lifeless figure.

'Don't you touch her,' Marian said, throwing herself between Lamar and Therese. 'Just let me take her with me.'

'She can't leave. She's lost her life and her death belongs here,' Lamar said. 'Now, I suggest you go before the Ones in The Blackness prevent it.'

'Come on, Marian. There's nothing we can do,' Jasper said.

'I won't leave her here,' Marian said. As the anger surged through her body once more, her light relit like a thousand-watt globe and the huddled horde was quick to respond. It pressed in on her, swallowing Therese with it as it tried to capture Marian.

'I'll be back for you – all of you,' Marian cried into the crowd.

She looked up, searching for the way out. The whirlpool opened above her head and she stretched her arms up towards it. It latched on to her, sucking her into its spinning vortex.

I'll be back, she promised herself, as she began to ascend.

Her heart was breaking and her mind was in chaos but all she knew was that she had to leave now so she could arm herself for her return. She needed something to fight with. As she rose, the air became sweeter and the cold was replaced by the warmth of home.

Chapter 39

Marian was released right back onto the bathroom floor. Her heart felt heavy. She dissolved into tears, thinking about how she would have to tell her father the news that the second woman he loved had met an early death.

Marian's thoughts then turned to her so-called ability and how it had created all this pain. She had tried to undo the havoc it had produced by entering The Grey Dusk but all she had achieved was the creation of a new catastrophe. And the way Gregory had run away showed he was no leader – no Lord Almighty.

I need to get Therese back. I need to get some help, Marian thought with renewed determination. But she had run out of time. Craig would have to know; there was no way to avoid it now. Cold hard reality waited to crash through their lives once again with a lightning speed that could destroy everything.

Marian heard a floorboard creak in the hallway outside the bathroom door. She whipped a towel off a nearby rail and threw it over the body.

'Are you both in there?' Craig said, tapping lightly on the bathroom door. 'You'd better get a move on; your dinner's getting cold.

'Dad, something terrible has happened,' Marian said, opening the door a crack. 'I tried to fix it. I tried to make it right.' She searched for the words, the right words, but there were none. She stepped aside to let her father see. She had no choice. She watched him as horror dawned and denial surfaced, both fighting for supremacy in his poor battered mind.

It was too much for Craig to bear. His body hit the cold, hard floor.

Marian reached out to grab him, to try to soften the fall. She remembered what her mother had always said about most household accidents happening in the bathroom. She would give anything to have her mother here right now. So much had changed in so little time.

Unconscious, at least Craig was able to catch a few moments of blessed oblivion. Marian folded a towel into a makeshift pillow and placed it gently between his head and the tiles. She slumped against the tub, watching the rhythmic rise and fall of his chest, as she tried to figure out what to do. She looked around the bathroom for Jasper, for Mina, for anyone, but she was alone with her unconscious father and her dead aunt.

I can't just sit here, Marian thought, jumping to her feet. She raced up to her room and threw open the balcony door.

'Wait,' Jasper said, appearing in the doorway.

'For what?' Marian said.

'For me.'

'This is as far as you go, Jasper. You can't ascend.'

'But I want to go with you.'

'Listen, I meant what I said to Gregory before he ran away. I think you're a good man on some level but I don't trust you – I don't trust any of you right now.'

* * *

Marian lifted her body, propelling it into the air, higher and higher, until she reached that magical place where sky-blue shades turned into spectacular magenta. She searched for Imogen as she scanned the lake's rim.

'You looked troubled, my dear,' Imogen said, when Marian found her sitting by the water's edge.

'Troubled – my God, I'm way past troubled. Haven't you seen what's been happening down there?'

Imogen nodded but her expression was far from sympathetic.

'I see you paid a visit to The Grey Dusk. You should never have gone down there.'

'Why? So I wouldn't find out about you and Gregory?'

'You took a great risk.'

'What was I supposed to do? Leave Therese there?' Marian's voice began to rise. It seemed Imogen wasn't going to help her.

'She's taken her own life. She's where she belongs.' Imogen folded her arms across her chest.

'She was under the influence of evil. She's innocent of any wrongdoing.' Marian felt her chest tighten with a seething hatred for Lamar.

'That may be so but she's trapped there nonetheless.'

'But we have to get her back!'

'She can't come back to life, Marian.'

A small crowd had gathered a short distance away, alerted by Marian's raised voice. They kept a respectful distance, a collective troubled look repeated on each face.

'She's right,' Mina said, separating herself from the crowd, venturing closer.

'I'm afraid so,' Margot said, also joining them. Her eyes filled with tears as she looked at this girl she loved so much. 'If there was anything we could do ...'

'So, I'm on my own,' Marian said, casting a disparaging look around the small group.

'None of us can venture there. Earth is as far as we can go,' Mina said, her own troubled eyes beseeching Marian's.

'I'll not leave Therese to a fate she doesn't deserve,' Marian said, as she began to float away.

'Marian, don't go back down there,' Margot called after her. But Marian barely heard her as she began to plan her next move.

* * *

Craig was still passed out on the bathroom floor when Marian returned from her wasted trip.

'Everything will be alright,' a voice said. It sounded like it was coming from the bath.

Marian peered over the edge but Therese remained still and lifeless. She looked at Craig sprawled out on the floor, quiet and still. She buried her face in her hands.

'Everything will be fine,' the same voice said, a little louder now.

'Shup up, just shut up,' Marian said, removing her hands from her face to cover her ears.

'Okay, that's enough of this,' the same voice spoke again.

Marian sensed the voice rather than heard it. She lowered her hands and looked for the source. 'Alright, I'm listening,' Marian said, getting to her feet. 'Where are you and what do you want?'

For a long moment there was silence. Marian waited for the voice to speak again. She squeezed her eyes shut and prayed that it would tell her what to do.

When she opened them, her eyes widened with a mixture of horror and fascination. Therese's body was *sitting up* in the bath. The face was still drawn and pale, stiff and lifeless, but as the body straightened up and stretched, it began to look more alive.

'I'll help you.' That same voice again. It was coming from Therese's mouth. It was almost comical the way the lips were moving as if they had never done so before. There was a look of astonishment on Therese's face as if she didn't quite believe what was happening.

The two women stared at each other in a silent standoff, neither sure of how much of what was happening was real.

'It's alright – it's okay,' Therese said, moving her lips awkwardly. The voice coming from Therese's mouth was not her own. It had an eerie resonance to it, like it was coming from far away. Marian almost joined her father on the floor but she was mesmerised by the sight of Therese's body coming back to life.

'You're not Therese. Who are you?' Marian said, edging closer to the reanimated body.

The Therese lookalike shook her head and looked down at her hands. 'These aren't mine,' she said, turning her hands over, examining them as if for the first time.

'Who *are* you?' Marian repeated.

Chapter 40

Gregory knew he had made the wrong decision as soon as he'd rejected Marian's light. He should have stayed where he was and stood his ground against her. The Grey Dusk was his! His kingdom and his rightful place. He had earned it. *I should never have let that slip of a girl rattle me the way she did*, he thought. But then he remembered the intensity of her light, the way it had opened his heart that had been long left closed and forgotten.

Fear quickly gave way to anger as he reached The Blackness. The ones there would be none-too-pleased to see him but he was almost beyond caring. A black peace had been his goal for centuries. Maybe now was his time to claim it.

His job was to oversee the torment and keep control of the souls not yet ready to take their final journey into this black abyss. His main goal was to control Marian and make her belong to them, to be on their side and join their cause. *I've made such a massive mess of it all,* Gregory thought, readying himself to face his betters. *But, what the hell …*

'I have no excuse,' Gregory said, throwing himself down on the sharp rocks, throwing himself on a mercy these beings didn't possess. 'I didn't anticipate the effect she would have on them.'

'You mean you didn't realise the effect she would have on *you*, Gregory,' a voice echoed from beyond the gate.

Wisps of black tendrils wound around the black bars, as Gregory waited to learn his punishment. Gregory had felt the black malevolence when he'd stood at the gate the first time, but there had been nothing to see. He expected this second occasion to be no different, until he saw a shape separate itself from the matt black behind the gate. It had no features; only an almost indiscernible ripple portrayed its separateness. Gregory focused on it, transfixed, watching it move as if it had been caught in a summer breeze. But there was nothing light and airy about it as he felt it watch him with its invisible eyes. As it came towards him, Gregory forced himself not to show his terror as he prepared to meet his fate.

'We may have underestimated the girl,' the ripple said. The voice was close and solid now; it had lost its menacing edge.

'Yes, she may be more powerful than even she herself knows,' Gregory said. He now realised he didn't want black peace. He wanted love. A smidge of his confidence restored, he continued. 'I've come for fresh instructions. New orders on how to handle the situation in light of these new developments.'

'You were not summoned; you had no permission to come before us.'

Gregory felt his small measure of confidence evaporate. The menacing edge had returned to the voice.

'Although we should keep you here, it suits our purpose to send you back.'

'Then may I go?' He could feel the heaviness of death here. He didn't want to add to it; he wanted to go back to his Grey Dusk, away from this place with no fire. He wouldn't let Marian see him run again. He'd find a way back to his fire, to his flaming crystal ball and his visions of Imogen.

'You are to go back to The Grey Dusk and wait for Marian to return. She ran, just as you did, in the face of the calamity her coming caused.'

'You mean she's not there?' Gregory had envisioned a new, white Grey Dusk filled with her light and her, the brightest shining star of all.

'She has gone but she will return. And when that time comes, you are to be ready for her. You are to quash her light. You are to control her and bring her before us.'

'I'll find a way,' Gregory said, bowing low from the waist. His relief was matched only by his fear of failure.

'Remember, we have Therese. You will keep her in The Grey Dusk until we have Marian, then you will bring her to join those here.'

After Gregory left, the Ones in The Blackness held counsel. They were not all agreed on letting Gregory return to The Grey Dusk after his epic failure. They had not all agreed on appointing him his position there in the first place. Some felt his remaining spark of goodness would be detrimental, while others felt it could enable him to secure Marian more easily.

'If she could learn to trust him, he could lead her here,' one said, 'then she will be ours.'

'You just want to live again,' another said, 'and this is how you think you will do it.'

A lost longing to escape had been reawakened somewhere down there in the dark. Everyone questioned everything since the coming of Marian. Her existence blurred the lines between life and death, and possibilities had surfaced that fanned long-lost, long-held desires. Marian could move between the spiritual planes, a power worth risking everything for, and these creatures of The Blackness wanted to possess it.

There were seven of these dead leaders, singularly nameless, collectively known as the Ones in The Blackness. Seven entities, united as one, joined in their separateness to rule and lead the souls who were buried down there with them.

They showed no mercy and no kindness to the souls in their keeping. The bad, the evil and the lost were all theirs for eternity – an army made ready to take over everything else in existence. They just needed Marian so they could escape. They wanted what she had, or at least the ability to control it.

'And of course, there is Imogen,' one said. 'Securing her would help enforce all our plans.' The leader of The Magenta Sky was a subject much discussed at every counsel. Having her under their control would secure them everything.

'Yes, that is the only reason I agreed to allow Gregory to go back,' another one of the seven said. 'His undying obsession with her will work well in our favour. If Marian can get Imogen to The Grey Dusk, we can do the rest.'

Chapter 41

'Where did you come from?' Marian said. 'Why are you here?' *Nothing's impossible,* she thought, as she watched the impossible unfold before her eyes

'I feel so strange,' the woman said.

'Okay, let's start from the beginning.'

Craig began to stir a little on the floor. A moan escaped his lips.

'Where's my baby?' the Therese double said. She suddenly grabbed her belly, a dawning horror replacing the confusion on her face. 'Where's my baby?'

'I don't know what's happened,' Marian said, placing a towel around the naked woman. 'But your baby's gone, along with your body.'

The woman stared at her and as Marian captured her gaze, she could see a scene playing out in their liquid depths. She could see a hospital room with a woman surrounded by the busyness of nurses. She had a huge belly and she was screaming in pain. The nurses were doing their best to comfort her, telling her that things would be alright. Marian realised that they were the same words she had just heard coming from Therese's mouth, almost like an echo from another world. This spirit had brought that echo with her to this one.

'I think you may have just died,' Marian said. She remembered what Glimmer had explained to her about the suddenness of death and the shock a soul went into when it was ripped from its body.

'No. This's just a bad dream. Yes that's it – that must be it.'

The words tore at Marian's heart. This spirit had tumbled into Therese's body – got lost along her way somehow. *Or maybe she hadn't. Maybe someone or something is trying to help me,* Marian thought.

'I need you to listen to me. I need you to trust me,' Marian said. 'Can you do that?'

'Okay – I'll try,' the spirit said as she looked around the unfamiliar bathroom. Her eyes rested on Craig lying prostrate on the tiles. 'Who's that?'

Marian knew she had very little time to salvage what she could from this situation. She knew her father would regain consciousness at any minute.

'We'll get to him later. What's the last thing you remember?' Marian said again. 'Do you know your name?'

'It's Christine, my name's Christine.' Marian saw the momentary satisfaction on Therese's face, as Christine remembered her name. 'And I remember the pain – there was so much blood.' The blank look of terror was slowly replaced by a crushing knowledge. 'My baby's gone. My little baby.' Christine cradled Therese's empty belly and rocked it back and forth.

'I promise I'll help you, but first I need to make you safe. See that man on the floor? He's my father and he loves you – I mean he loves the woman he *thinks* you are.'

Christine opened Therese's mouth to speak but Marian placed her index finger up to her lips. 'I'll try and find out what happened to you and your baby but first I need you to pretend to be the woman that man loved.'

Forgetting her distress for the moment, Christine admired the good-looking man sprawled out on the tiles. Then she thought of her baby's father – a no-good one-night stand who wanted nothing to do with fatherhood.

'I-I'll try. What do you want me to do?'

'I don't want my father to know that she's dead – not yet.'

Craig's eyes fluttered open and he tried to sit up. He looked at the two women staring at him and he forced himself into a sitting position.

'What happened?' he said, struggling to get to his feet. Marian could see the shock and denial still lingering on his face.

'Honestly, what am I going to do with you two? I can't leave either of you alone for five minutes,' Marian said. 'One slips in the bath and the other does the same on the wet floor. Are you alright, Dad?' She could see his physicality was intact but his mind was another story.

'Are you okay, Therese?' Craig said. He looked hard at her, scarcely daring to believe that the woman he loved was alive and breathing. He was sure he'd seen her stone-cold dead in the bath.

Christine didn't know this man or this girl but she let them help her stand up. As she stepped from the bath, Christine caught a glimpse of her own reflection in the bathroom mirror. She didn't know her either.

'What happened? Are you alright?' Craig said as he wrapped her robe around her.

'I don't remember. I don't remember anything,' Christine said. She glanced at Marian, taking the almost indiscernible nod as a sign that she'd made an acceptable response.

Craig's face showed his anguish as he held Therese close. *He really does love her,* Marian thought, noticing his distorted features.

Craig ran his hand lovingly through Therese's hair. Christine sat very still, putting up no resistance, allowing him free rein of Therese's body. He searched for any tell-tale lumps and bumps on her head before he ran his hands down her arms and legs to check for any possible injury. Water began to leak from Therese's nose where she'd inhaled it into her lungs as she died but Christine was quick to wipe it away on the towel before Craig noticed.

'Help your aunt get dressed and I'll go and call the doctor.'

The three of them nodded in unison. It was a way to move forward, out of this bathroom and back into the world.

Chapter 42

'This way,' Marian whispered, leading Christine down the hall to the bedroom. There was a full-length mirror on the wall. Christine stopped in front of it and studied the reflection she saw there.

'I don't understand any of this. How can this be happening?' She touched her unfamiliar face and hair. She turned to look at the rest of her new body. An appreciative smile began to play on her full lips. 'I'm really a very plain girl – not a beauty like this.'

'Yes, Therese is beautiful,' Marian said, looking at Christine. 'I mean, she was.' Tears stung Marian's eyes as she examined Therese's shell.

Christine stared at Therese's body in the mirror, her baby all but forgotten. The one-night stand that had produced a baby without a father had no place in this new world Christine had tumbled into. 'If this isn't a dream, then I've fallen off the other side of reality,' she said.

'I want you to tell me what you know,' Marian said, trying to tear Christine away from Therese's reflection. 'At least tell me who you are, I mean, who you were.'

Christine absently ran Therese's hands over the things on the dressing table, selecting a large hair brush. She picked it up so she could brush the long hair on Therese's head.

'I always wanted hair like this – mine's short and wiry.' The smile widened on Christine's new face. 'I'm so pretty – just look at me.' She stopped brushing Therese's hair and stared into the mirror again.

'Christine, listen to me. We need to work out a plan.'

'Oh, I already have *my* plan,' Christine said, opening the wardrobe door and seeing the delights it held. 'I'm gone, my baby's gone and however it happened, I'm here now.'

'My father's just lost the woman he loves,' Marian said. 'He doesn't know it yet and I want to try and find a way to spare him any more pain.' Marian touched the face that was staring back at her through the mirror. 'This is Therese. She's my aunt.'

'Your aunt?' Christine asked. 'I thought she was your mother.'

'Yes, my aunt. She and my father are very much in love. Their shared grief at my mother's death brought them closer together.'

'So you're telling me that when your mother died, her sister took your father for herself? Sounds to me like she made the best of the situation.'

'It wasn't like that. They didn't plan it.'

'She went after him, alright. She got to him when he was hurt and vulnerable. She probably always wanted him. Her own sister's husband.'

Marian could see past Therese's exterior to the woman inside. She was raw and honest, saying exactly what she thought. Marian couldn't help but admire her.

'I wonder where she is now?' Christine said. 'Where's her soul gone?'

Marian was ashamed to tell her the truth but there was something about Christine that she trusted.

'She killed herself to be with a dead man.'

'She what?' Christine forgot about her reflection as she whipped her head away from the mirror. 'I thought she was in love with your father.'

'Her heart was possessed by this man – a spirit. He wouldn't let her go. She's now in The Grey Dusk, a place where souls linger in the gloom awaiting their final step into The Blackness. I need to get her back. I can't leave her down there.'

Marian's tears began to fall and Christine comforted this compelling stranger as best she could. 'Maybe she deserves to be where she is,' she said quietly. She thought Therese sounded greedy and selfish.

'No, no-one deserves that fate.' Marian shivered as she thought of the doom and gloom, the desperation and the despair on the faces of the lost souls. 'I have to get her back. And I have to save the others.'

'I'll help you.' Christine would do anything to stay in Therese's body.

Chapter 43

'I've made an appointment with Dr Emery for later today,' Craig said when Marian and Christine came into the kitchen. 'I like the way you've done your hair, Therese.' He admired the new style, his concern momentarily forgotten. Christine blushed, delighted he'd noticed. 'How do you feel now?'

'Do you have any coffee?' Christine asked as Craig handed her a cup of tea.

Craig nearly dropped the cup. 'Since when do you drink coffee?' He looked at Therese and his concern amplified. 'I think we'll forget the doctor; we're going to the hospital.' He poured his tea down the sink and grabbed his car keys. 'Come on – in the car.' The look on his face left no room for argument.

'Going to the hospital's a good idea,' Marian said as she took Christine to find Therese's handbag. 'We should get Therese's body checked out. She *was* dead for a while before you brought her back to life.'

'I brought *myself* back to life, Marian.'

'How do you know my name?' Marian knew she hadn't told her and her father hadn't uttered it since he'd regained consciousness.

'I don't know. Someone must have told me.'

'Who? Who told you?'

'I told you, I don't know.' Christine opened Therese's wardrobe again and ran her hands over the neat, expensive row of handbags nestled on the top shelf.

'Come on, Dad's waiting,' Marian said.

* * *

'We'll go in my car,' Craig said, noticing Therese's hesitation and her indecision as they walked outside. His alarm increased as he realised she didn't remember anything. They drove in silence with Craig keeping a close eye on Therese.

Marian sat in the back seat, glad for a few minutes to herself. She was anxious to find some answers. She wanted to know how what had happened was even possible. Since she had started working at the shop with Celia, where all sorts, alive or dead, came to call with their questions and their unfinished business, Marian had never heard of this. Even at the psychic fair where Therese had met Lamar and become possessed by him, there was still a distinct line between the living and the dead.

Marian closed her eyes and saw Jasper, the spirit who had captured her attention and her heart that same day. She thought about how he'd been there to help and guide her following her discovery in the bathroom. He'd shown her the way to The Grey Dusk where he'd been languishing, unwilling to step into The Blackness. She remembered the almost desperate plea in his eyes for help to remain earthbound, the good in him winning the struggle against the bad. And she felt her heart twist in pain as she thought of her failure to get Therese back. *He must have sent Christine. Who else would have?'* Marian thought.

Marian felt a presence fill the space next to her in the back seat. She opened her eyes and looked straight into Margot's merry old eyes.

'I don't want you to worry, my dear. You are not alone – you're never alone.'

'This all started with you,' Marian whispered, remembering the day Margot had died, when Marian could still see Margot in her rocking chair on her patio long after the ambulance had taken her body away. 'I didn't ask for any of this.' She could feel tears threatening behind her eyes and the weight of the responsibility on her shoulders.

'I know, my dear, I know. It chose you.'

'Did you have anything to do with sending Christine's spirit?'

'No, but I think you did.'

'But I had nothing to do with it!'

'You're becoming more aware – more complete. You just may have bought yourself some time.' Margot smiled and melted into the backseat just as the car pulled up at the hospital emergency entrance.

* * *

'I can't seem to find a thing wrong. All the test results are normal,' the treating doctor said after his initial examination of Therese was complete.

'So what do you think may be causing this sudden amnesia?' Craig said.

'She's physically unharmed?' Marian interrupted, relieved to know that Therese's body had been pronounced intact.

'As I was saying, I can find nothing physically wrong with her but I'd like to keep her overnight for observation, just to be on the safe side.'

'We can take care of her at home,' Marian interrupted again, not wanting to leave Christine here by herself.

'Whatever you think's best. Thank you, Doctor,' Craig said staring at Therese who only seemed interested in her reflection in the big silver examination light above the bed.

'We'll keep a close eye on her here. I'll organise a psychiatric consult for her should the amnesia persist.'

Marian almost burst out laughing. *If only he knew,* she thought.

'We could bring her back for that,' Marian said.

'I want to keep her here in case her condition worsens. We'll take good care of her.'

'Marian, Therese is staying and that's that,' Craig said.

'Now, she needs her rest,' the doctor said. 'I'll leave you to say your goodbyes.' The doctor smiled and proceeded to the nurse's station with the patient's chart that said: *Sudden, unexplained amnesia. No apparent physical cause. For psych consult if unresolved. Admitted for observation.*

* * *

'What's happened to Therese?' Craig said to Marian as they put their seatbelts on. 'She's acting so abnormal – amnesia or not.'

'I don't know,' Marian mumbled, unable to meet Craig's eyes. The tension began to grow as Craig drove out of the emergency car park.

'You never were a good liar, even for the best of reasons.'

'I don't want you to get hurt. You've been through so much.'

'And you haven't? My God, Marian! Look at us … this isn't normal.'

'What's normal anyway?'

'Well, certainly not this. I have a daughter who's made of magic who won't let me help her, and now Therese who doesn't know who she is. You're not going through this alone, Marian. You're never alone.'

'That's what Margot said.'

Chapter 44

Christine lay awake long after Marian and Craig left. She was back in hospital again in a different body with a different problem. She challenged her own sanity as she gazed at her new reflection in the examination light for at least the hundredth time that night. Sleep escaped her as she wondered what kind of being she now was, with her own body dead and the owner of this one gone God knows where. She couldn't leave but she didn't feel trapped. She was where she was supposed to be. That's all she was sure of right now.

'You really wanted that baby. I saw it in your dead eyes.'

'Who said that?' Christine whispered into the dark. She pulled the covers tightly around Therese's body.

'Someone who's trying to help you.' There was a faint movement at the end of the bed as a silhouette began to appear.

Christine tried to focus on the emerging form as it came closer. 'What do you want? How do you know about my baby?'

'Because I was there. I sent you here.'

Christine bit down on Therese's bottom lip to stifle a scream. 'What have you done with my baby?'

'We had no use for him so we let him go – you know – to rest in peace. You'll see him again when you're ready for your own rest.'

Christine felt the tears roll down Therese's face as she imagined her little boy. 'You saved my life?'

'Well, not exactly. I didn't waste your death.'

Christine released the grip Therese had on the covers. 'Who are you? What do you want from me?'

'My name's Elizabeth and I'm here to be a part of the greatest rebirth imaginable. There are things unfolding – great things. I'm offering you a part in that.'

Christine gazed at her own reflection, falling more and more in love with what she saw. 'What do you want me to do?'

'I need you to take care of Therese – of her body.' Christine nodded, eager to please, dying to hear more. 'Marian is the prize. She's the beginning and the end to all of this …'

* * *

'Ready to go?' Marian said the next morning. She'd left Craig outside trying to find a car park. Marian was eager for a few minutes alone with Christine.

She'd lain awake all night too, trying to figure out how she could make this situation with Christine work until Therese came back. *I need Imogen – she'll know what to do,* she thought. Around 3.00 am she gave up trying to sleep and went up to The Magenta Sky to have it out with her.

'But if Gregory was here, that means travel *is* possible between the realms,' Marian said. They'd talked it all out and Marian understood that Imogen had only been trying to save Gregory's soul. Falling in love with him had been an unforeseen complication in the process, making Gregory's inevitable dismissal heartbreaking for her.

'That must have been so hard, sending Gregory away like that,' Marian said when she'd heard the whole story.

'Yes, but when he showed his true colours, and they were mostly grey and black, I had no choice.' The pain dimmed the sparkle in Imogen's eyes as she remembered. 'Never mix business with pleasure.' She attempted a smile but her eyes welled with tears.

'It's a bit like Henry and me.' Marian remembered the way her stomach had turned over whenever she saw him. *But that was before Jasper,* she thought.

'Love has no rhyme or reason. The heart wants want the heart wants,' Imogen said. 'And it seems it never dies, just as the soul lives on.'

Marian thought about Therese's heart and how it had led to her demise. 'I guess you're right.'

'But enough of this, we have problems to solve. You're growing more aware – becoming more complete.'

'That's what Margot said.'

'Yes, she's a wise old thing for someone so young.'

'You mean because she's only been dead for a short time?'

'That's right. She's not an old-timer like me.'

'Therese's only been dead for a little while. There must be something we can do.'

Imogen shook her head. 'It's true, there *is* room to move between realms in extreme cases but Therese's situation is different. No-one comes back from the dead.'

'And no-one can exist with the dead while they're still living either.'

Imogen nodded, smiling at Marian's serious face. 'Yes, except for you.'

'Then I'll not give up on getting Therese back.' She gave Imogen one last frown before returning to her bed and her sleepless night.

* * *

'So, are you ready to go?' Marian asked Christine again.

'Yes, I had a dreadful night … and a visitor.'

'Who?' Marian was almost afraid to ask.

'Someone who didn't want to see my death wasted.'

Craig arrived then with a smile and a bunch of flowers. 'I've just spoken with the doctor and he's happy to release you into my care,' he said. 'He seems to think your memory will come back in time and I have the psychiatrist's referral right here.' Craig brandished a crisp, white envelope in his hand. 'How are you feeling this morning? Do you remember anything?'

'Only that I love you – both of you.'

Craig saw a conspiratorial look exchanged between Therese and Marian. He was determined to get to the bottom of what was going on. He'd had a bad night himself — a nightmare full of loss and longing. 'Well, let's get you home,' he said. They went out to the car park with Craig leading the way.

'Who didn't want to waste your death?' Marian whispered.

'She said her name was Elizabeth and she said I was a part of some great rebirth or something.'

'What else did she say?' Marian's heart began to hammer in her chest as she tried to imagine what this could mean. But Christine had quickened her pace to catch up with Craig. *She's only interested in her new body,* Marian thought, watching her flutter Therese's eyelashes at her father.

Chapter 45

'Where's Therese?' Craig said, hovering over the teapot. He'd delivered them all safely home and now he was on duty in the kitchen.

'She's upstairs resting,' Marian said. That wasn't strictly true. Christine was lost in Therese's wardrobe, trying on clothes. 'Um ... Dad, that's not Therese up there.'

'What are you talking about?' Craig said, the teapot shaking slightly in his hands.

Marian took it from him then sat down at the kitchen table. 'Sit down, I'll try to explain ...' Then she launched into a lengthy explanation of all that had happened.

'So, you think we can get her back?' Craig said when Marian had finished.

'Get who back?' Christine said from the doorway.

'Therese,' Craig said, 'we're talking about Therese, Christine.'

'Marian! You told him. Why?'

'He needed to know the whole story,' Marian said, standing between her and Craig. 'He had already worked some of it out.'

'Well, it's not as though either of you can do anything about it,' Christine said, picking up the teapot. 'I think I'm developing a taste for this.'

'Listen, Christine, I need you to tell me about Elizabeth. What else did she tell you?' Marian said.

'She told me to take good care of Therese's body.' Christine stroked Therese's face.

'I'm not sure of this Elizabeth; she's not known in The Magenta Sky,' Marian said.

'So she must work for the other side,' Craig said.

'I'm a good person,' Christine said. 'I never did anything wrong. All my life people have taken advantage of me – treated me like I didn't matter. This is the best thing that's ever happened to me.'

'And we're very grateful for your help but we still need to get Therese back,' Craig said.

'But what happens if you can't?' Christine said, tears forming in Therese's eyes.

'I don't know. We'll have to wait and see.' Her meaning wasn't lost on Craig but he couldn't conceive of the idea of replacing Therese with Christine.

'I think it's time to gather our friends – see who we can count on,' Marian said.

'I don't want you travelling to that Grey Dusk place alone, Marian. It's not safe,' Craig said.

'Christine, I want you to tell me if Elizabeth appears to you again. Tell her I want to talk to her,' Marian said, ignoring her father's plea. 'Now, I have to get to work.'

* * *

The bell tinkled as Marian entered the shop. She let the feeling of safety wash over her for a moment before pulling her mind back to her dilemma.

'Good morning, Marian,' Celia said, looking up from the counter. 'You look like Hell. What's wrong?'

'I'm sorry I couldn't make it to work yesterday. Something happened. Are we expecting Glimmer today?' Marian said, waving away Celia's concern.

'She's out the back trying to talk to Heston.'

Marian couldn't help but smile at Glimmer's dedication. If she could, Glimmer would lead the charge into The Grey Dusk and save them all. 'There are a few things I need to talk to you two about – unbelievable things.'

Celia's heart raced as Marian flipped the sign on the shop door over. She wondered what they were going to hear next. 'I hope we won't have to be closed for long,' she said.

Marian wandered through the shop, parting the amber beaded curtain leading to the back. Celia followed closely behind. Glimmer was already there, talking through the open window to a patient-looking Heston.

'He can hear you. He's looking right at you,' Marian said.

Glimmer turned to Marian, her face alight with excitement. 'I just wish I had the gift you have,' she said.

'You may not feel that way when I've finished saying what I have to say. Heston, what do you know about Elizabeth?'

Celia and Glimmer looked from Marian to the window and back at each other. They sat down, waiting for Marian to reveal this new situation.

'My sole purpose is to watch over Celia, and now you. I'm not privy to the activities of The Magenta Sky or anywhere else for that matter,' Heston said.

Marian let out a defeated sigh and sat down with Celia and Glimmer. She could see the concern reflected in their loving faces as she prepared herself to shatter their worlds.

'Therese is dead. She killed herself – drowned herself in the bath,' Marian said.

The other two women jumped to their feet in shock and surprise.

'What? Why?' Glimmer said, the first to find her voice.

'Chasing a ghost,' Marian said.

'Ghost. What ghost?' Celia said.

'Sit down and I'll try to explain. You remember the incident at the fair when Therese ran off through the crowd? The way she acted? That's where it began.'

Celia and Glimmer held their breath, waiting for Marian to continue.

'Well, she chased him all the way to death and I don't know how to bring her back. And by the way, it seems I have greater power than we first thought.' Marian stood up and drifted toward the ceiling, pacing through the air. 'I can go all the way to Heaven and down to Hell, if I so choose.'

Glimmer and Celia were silent for a few moments, trying to process what Marian was saying.

'Could you come down here?' Celia said. 'It's hard to hear you from up there.'

Marian descended to floor-level and resumed her pacing. 'I've been to look for her but they had her in some enforced isolation. They called it settling in.' Marian abruptly stopped her pacing and looked at the two women. 'I know this sounds insane – looks insane, but I swear I'm telling you the truth.'

'I don't doubt it for a minute,' Glimmer said.

'I want to tell you all of it. I need to. There's The Magenta Sky and a place called The Grey Dusk …'

'You can't go back down there,' Heston said through the open window. 'It's too dangerous.'

'Jasper will be with me. I only need to whisper his name and he'll appear.'

'But he's one of them,' Heston said, his usual serene features contorting in anger. 'No-one enters The Grey Dusk unless they have a dark soul.'

'I did. Do I have a dark soul? We all harbour a smidgen of evil within us. We possess free will, even after death, to follow a path of enlightenment or one of endarkenment. Nothing's final until our soul decides where it wants to reside for eternity.'

Glimmer and Celia exchanged another look, trying to understand the one-sided conversation.

'That may be so, but you can't put yourself in danger for what may be,' Heston said.

'I want to help Jasper,' Marian said. 'There's good in him. I can see it in his eyes.'

'And what about Raven? Did you see the deceit in hers?'

Marian fell silent as she thought about the lies that had slipped so easily through Raven's lips.

'I trusted her,' Marian whispered, hanging her head as the tears began to fall.

'You see the good in all of us but you need to be able to read the bad,' Glimmer said, beginning to follow the conversation.

'You have such a burden to carry,' Celia said, her own tears falling.

'I told you it's not a gift,' Marian said.

'Gift or not, it's been bestowed on you and we're here to help and protect you,' Glimmer said, more certain than ever of the part she was destined to play.

Marian looked at all three of them, her eyes shining with tears and love for them all.

Chapter 46

'Are you sure this is a good idea? A séance can be dangerous,' Celia said.

'The room looks perfect,' Glimmer said, ignoring Celia's concern. She fluttered around, moving this candle and that while they waited for everyone to arrive. There were to be four others besides themselves and Marian.

'Are we all set?' Marian said, parting the beaded curtain. Her eyes locked with Heston's concerned ones as he stood on guard outside the window. 'What's the matter?' she asked him.

'We need to be wary and cautious. Uninvited guests will arrive along with the invited ones,' he said.

'Look, I agreed not to go back to The Grey Dusk to look for Therese. Glimmer thinks this may work, that she might come to us. I'm not giving up, Heston.'

The old soldier nodded before melting into the twilight. Marian leant on the windowsill, breathing in the early evening air. She looked up at the last traces of pink streaking across the sky. 'Wish me luck,' she whispered.

'We're ready, Marian,' Glimmer said, gently touching her elbow. Marian turned to see all eyes in the room trained on her.

'Oh, I'm sorry; I must have been miles away.' Marian took her seat at the table. She cast her eyes around at the odd gathering. Celia was sitting to her right, her eyes darting around the room as if she was preparing herself to tackle a ghost. Glimmer was sitting on her left, anticipation and excitement giving her face an ethereal glow. A man in a dark suit bowed his head slightly as he met Marian's gaze. There was a younger man sitting next to him who shared the same facial features and sombre expression. *They must be father and son,* Marian thought, as she moved on to the next guest. A woman with gypsy earrings and a multi-coloured scarf sat next to the younger man, and a wizened old lady completed the group.

'I would like to thank you all for coming,' Glimmer said.

'I recognise you from the psychic fair,' Marian said, addressing the old lady. She realised these were the higher minds that Glimmer had mentioned.

'Yes, I was there. My name is Clara and I'm very humbled to be included in our little group this evening.'

'And I'm Michael and this is my son Eddie,' the older man said.

'My name's Anthea,' the lady with the gypsy earrings said. 'I'm so pleased to be here.'

Marian smiled nervously at everyone around the table. 'I hope you can help me. I'm very grateful you've all come here this evening.'

The table began to vibrate as if a current of electricity was running through it, causing Celia to topple off her chair.

'It's alright. They're just anxious for us to get started,' Clara said.

Anthea got up from the table and righted Celia's chair. 'Please take your seat, Celia,' Anthea said, placing her hand on Celia's arm and gently guiding her back to the table.

'We've created an abundance of energy in this room,' Michael said, his hands resting on the table were trembling.

'Is that a good thing?' Marian said, feeling the current from the table run through her own fingers.

'It means we're in for one hell of a show,' Eddie said, drumming his hands on the table top.

'Please everyone, join hands,' Michael said, extending his own, noting the surprise on Marian's face. 'Yes, Marian, I'm the master of ceremonies.'

They did as they were asked, creating an unbroken circle of hands around the quivering table.

Marian felt a tugging on her sleeve. 'You should be running this show,' a little boy said.

'Oh, I don't think so. I've never done this before,' Marian said, smiling at him. 'Is there something I can do for you?'

'I just wanted to tell you, your mother's watching.'

Before Marian could open her mouth to speak, the little boy vanished. Marian looked at the faces staring at her. She snatched her hands back, breaking the circle.

'My mother can see me. How's that possible?' All thoughts of Therese left Marian's mind at the mention of Sonia.

'I tried to warn you about unwanted guests,' Heston said from the window, raising his voice to be heard.

Marian hurried over to him with renewed hope in her heart. 'But what if she *can* see me?' Marian said, leaning on the windowsill.

'That's not possible. Sonia's gone to her paradise.'

'But what if she wants to come back?'

Heston shook his head sadly. 'There *is* no coming back once The Paradise is entered and I daresay the same rules apply down below.' He retreated back into the shadows.

Marian swung around to face the room of shocked faces. Only Glimmer remained composed as the others stared at her in wonder.

'I told you she was spectacular,' Glimmer said.

'I'm sorry for the interruption. I'd like to continue now,' Marian said, taking her place back in the circle.

'I'd like to offer you my place,' Michael said, bowing his head. 'You have greatness in you and I would like to help you learn how to use it.'

They all joined hands again, looking towards Marian with unbridled anticipation.

'I'd like to ask my mother, Sonia White, to join us,' Marian said, closing her eyes.

Glimmer opened her mouth to speak but was stunned into silence as the table began to lift off the ground. Chairs were forced back, out of the rising table's way. A collective gasp escaped those witnessing Marian's ascension as she rose with the table.

'Are you here, Mum?' Marian's eyes darted back and forth across the ceiling, searching for a sign.

'She can't come, Marian – you know that,' Mina said, suddenly materialising in the room.

'That's right, she's at peace now, unaware of events outside her paradise,' Margot said, appearing next to Mina.

'I'm sorry, Marian – you're my only true friend,' Raven said, also appearing by Marian's side.

'There's nothing true about you, Raven. You're nothing but a scheming liar. I'll never forgive you.'

'But I thought you wanted to help those trapped in The Grey Dusk? I'm trapped.'

'And you have Therese trapped in there with you. Where is she?'

Down below, the others watched Marian as she carried on a conversation with invisible beings. 'I can't believe I'm seeing this,' Clara said. 'She's conducting her own séance up there.'

'I don't think so. She's just talking with those she knows,' Eddie said. 'Makes us all look like a bunch of amateurs.'

'But we're witnessing a true miracle tonight and I for one will pledge the rest of my life to her,' Anthea said.

'As will we all,' Michael said.

Chapter 47

'Any luck?' Craig said as Marian came through the front door. He'd been waiting up for her, anxious to know if she'd been able to contact Therese.

'They're holding her hostage.' Marian sat down next to Craig on the lounge and put her head on his shoulder. 'I think Mum was there.'

'What? How's that possible?' Craig jumped to his feet, nearly knocking Marian off the lounge.

'I don't know but I received a message.' Marian moved from the lounge to the window. She gazed up at the sky and wondered.

'Did you try and talk to her?'

'They all said her concerns with this world are over but I don't know …'

'I'm still here,' Christine said, venturing into the room. 'I've been sitting upstairs, waiting for Therese to come and claim her body, but I guess the evening was less than a success.'

'Yes, for us,' Marian said. 'You must be happy, though.'

'I didn't ask for any of this, Marian. It's not my fault that Therese killed herself. In fact, if it wasn't for me, this body would be rotting in the ground about now.'

'And we thank you for being its caretaker,' Craig said, smiling at her. 'I don't know if I can ever forgive her for what she's done.'

'How can you say that? She was under a spell,' Marian said.

'That may be so but it doesn't change anything,' Craig said, directing his words at Christine.

'If she wasn't guilty, she wouldn't be down there,' Christine said.

Craig looked hard at her and nodded.

'So what do you want me to do – leave her there?' Marian said.

'I don't see that you have much of a choice. Therese made hers. Come on, Christine. Let's call it a night.'

'Please call me Therese – let me be Therese,' Christine said, beseeching Craig with her eyes.

'You're not Therese, Christine,' Marian said. 'I'll get her back and then we'll decide what we're going to do with you.'

* * *

Marian sat out on her balcony gazing up at the stars. Sleep eluded her as she sat deep in thought.

'A penny for them,' Jasper said, separating from the dark.

'Can't you read my mind?' Marian said, a sad smile on her lips.

'No, not one of my talents, but if I could hazard a guess, I'd say that you have no idea what to do.'

'Or who to trust,' Marian said, her smile turning into a frown.

'Therese is out of isolation. Gregory released her.'

'So he came crawling back. I'll bet Lamar was pleased about that.'

'There was a momentary show of strength but the Ones in The Blackness reinstated Gregory as lord and master, dissolving Lamar, adding him to their growing horde of souls.'

'I still need to get Therese back.'

'She followed Lamar. As soon as Gregory broke her chains, she tore after him. I'm sorry Marian but she's gone.'

'So she really did want to be with him.' The tears tracked down Marian's face as she realised that there had been no real spell.

'There's nothing you can do for her now.'

'What do you know about The Blackness, Jasper?'

'It's a place to exist outside existence where a soul can become one with the many.'

'Therese didn't deserve that fate. She was only chasing a ghost. And what about you, what fate do you deserve?'

'I committed crimes while I was alive. I fed souls to the Devil.'

'What?'

'I was a psychic but I broke all the rules. If I could do it all again, I wouldn't make the same mistakes.'

'And what caused this change of heart?'

'You. You did. The way you shone your light into that grey landscape, the way they turned to you, the way they reached for you. I want to be part of that light.'

'But that wasn't always so, was it?'

'No, I admit I was recruited to capture you, to capture your heart and deliver you to Gregory, but you've captured mine and delivered me from evil.'

'How can I believe a thing you say, any of you? Raven lied to me my whole life.'

Marian launched herself away from him, up into the starry sky. *Things are so messed up down there,* she thought as The Magenta Sky came into view. As her feet came to rest on the ground, the familiar feeling of peace wrapped itself around her hurting heart. She sat down by the edge of the lake and let the feeling soothe her.

'You have the troubles of the world on your shoulders,' Margot said, positioning herself by Marian's side.

'I wish we could go back to your house and you could make lemonade for me,' Marian sighed.

'I know, my dear, I know.'

'You're the only one I can trust.'

'Oh, there are others, you just need to forgive them. Imogen was only trying to show Gregory a better way but he chose otherwise. They fell in love, a bit like you and Jasper are doing now.' Marian opened her mouth to protest, but Margot held her hand up to silence her. 'It's the internal struggle with the good and the bad. One side has to win in the end.'

'So, Therese has chosen?'

'I think the decision was made for her.'

'So, she could come back?'

'Rules are made to be broken and this has never been more apparent where you are concerned. Look at you! Alive and well with the living and the dead. Your very existence challenges everything we thought we knew.'

'So, we're all in this together.'

'You'll be the one who *makes* the rules.'

Marian shook her head as she got to her feet. 'I'm not worthy of this.'

'Well, you're the only one who thinks so.'

'Really? Then it's about time I stretched my wings, so to speak.'

'Good girl. Embrace it. It really is a gift.'

'Then, I want to see my mother.'

Chapter 48

Marian could see bright orbs of light dancing through the gate. The place was one of total serenity. A perfect end for the souls who were ready for their eternity.

'Have you been here before?' Marian asked Imogen standing beside her.

'Yes, when the safe-keeping of The Magenta Sky was granted to me.'

'Did you want the job?'

'I wasn't ready for paradise. I felt there was still much for me to do, and of course, I had to wait for you.'

'I'm sorry I said I couldn't trust you. Look what you've given up for me.'

'It was all part of you coming to understand – coming to look beyond what's shown on the surface.'

'I can see more with my eyes closed now.' Imogen smiled and touched Marian on the arm. 'And I can feel your touch, solid and reassuring.'

'We're living beings to you now. You can touch us, feel us and take us into your heart.'

'I still expect to wake up from this dream but I don't want to,' Marian said, as she watched the orbs of light dance around in their absolute serenity.

'Look, here comes the lightkeeper.'

Marian became entranced as she watched an orb separate itself from the others and glide towards the gate. As it came closer, Marian could see features develop through the light. The orb became a man, tall and majestic, gliding effortlessly towards them. He stood just behind the gate, his face wreathed in smiles.

'Is that God?' Marian whispered, falling to her knees.

'Arise, my child. It is I who should kneel before you. I am merely the custodian of the light. I bestow it on those who enter their paradise. My name is Midas.'

'Like in, "The Midas touch"?' Marian stood up, marvelling at this celestial being.

'Yes, only everything I touch turns to pure light,' Midas said.

Marian beamed back at him despite the serious question she was about to ask.

'And how are you, Imogen?' Midas said. 'The Pure Souls have been watching the developments with the greatest of interest.'

'It's good to see you, Midas. Yes, things have certainly been turned upside down since the arrival of this little treasure.'

'You are the only living soul to ever stand at Paradise Gate,' Midas said solemnly. 'This place is run by The Pure Ones, seven souls who have reached complete enlightenment. Those who dwell here are at complete peace – no cares or ties to the world below.'

'I wish I could just talk to her – my mother – even for a minute. I miss her so much,' Marian said, a single tear making its sad journey down her cheek. 'It's been so hard without her – so much has happened.' She looked longingly through the bars of the gate, willing her mother to appear.

'The Pure Ones must have made an exception,' Midas said as he watched the progress of a stray orb that had become separate from the dance. It zig-zagged towards the gate, alighting on Midas's outstretched palm.

'Come, little one, be as you were.'

'Mum!' Marian whispered, as the metamorphosis of the orb was completed.

'It's alright, Sonia,' Midas said. 'Look who's here.'

Sonia turned from him and stared at Marian through the bars of light. 'Marian, oh my Marian.' She turned back to Midas. 'Is she dead?'

'No, she's just amazingly special,' Midas said.

'I never thought I'd see you before death, Marian. How can you be here?'

'I have the ability to be anywhere, it seems.'

Sonia reached through the bars of the gate, touching Marian's hands gently. 'Open the gate, Midas,' Sonia pleaded.

'I'm sorry, Sonia. This gate can only open one way for you. You'll have to wait until it's Marian's turn to pass through it.'

'Are you alright, Marian? Why are you here?' Sonia said.

'I only wanted to see you – to tell you that I love you.' Marian squeezed Sonia's hands tight. *I can't tell her,* she thought. 'Did you come to the séance?'

'As I have said, those that pass through this gate have no ties to the world below,' Midas interrupted.

'But it seems I have ties to this one,' Marian said.

Sonia smiled and blew Marian a kiss as a light began to illuminate her body from within. Her body became one with it as she orbed gently away from the gate.

'You may come and visit again – if The Pure Ones allow it,' Midas said softly.

Imogen held Marian close. 'You were very brave,' she said.

'I saw no reason to burden her with what's happened. I sent enough of a ripple through her paradise as it was, and you know what they say about the ripple effect …'

'Your mother will suffer no ill effects from your visit. The Pure Ones will ensure that,' Midas said. His features began to distort as the light now reclaimed his body and orbed him gracefully away.

'I think she's happy,' Marian said to Imogen as they took their leave.

'Midas will watch over her for you.'

'Do you think the gate leading into The Blackness has similar rules to Paradise Gate?'

'If it wasn't a one-way gate, havoc would rule the earth. I think I can safely say, that once a soul has passed through, there is no chance of return.'

'Then, Therese really is gone.'

Imogen nodded sadly and reached for Marian's hand. 'You're not to blame yourself.'

'But if I didn't keep insisting that she remember … if I'd only left her in blissful ignorance, her eyes would have remained closed to this world. She would never have seen Lamar and she would be safe and sound at home.' Marian began to cry in earnest as The Magenta Sky came into view. 'If she must be dead, she should at least be here with us.'

A crowd began to gather around them as they landed on the soft ground by the lake.

'What happened?' Mina said.

'Now's not a good time,' Imogen said, waving the crowd away. Mina's face dropped as she turned to go. 'Not you, Mina – Marian needs you.'

'I saw her, I saw my mother, Mina. It's the most beautiful place I've ever seen. All light and bright, and watched over by the kindest of souls.'

'Then why are you crying?' Mina said gently.

'Because Therese is trapped in an opposite place and I can't help her.' Anger and frustration forced Marian's tears away as she began pacing by the water's edge. 'I don't care what anyone says, Lamar possessed her.'

'If that's so, then she truly doesn't belong there.'

'Of course she doesn't belong there. It's a miscarriage of justice.'

'So what are you going to do?'

'I'll tell you what I'm going to do. I'll pound on that black gate, until they let her out.'

Chapter 49

'I've been warned not to go but I must,' Marian said.

'Then, I'll go with you,' Jasper said.

'No, you'll only be able to go as far as The Grey Dusk. I'll have to take the rest of the journey alone.'

'But how will you know how to get there?'

'They want me there, those black devils. I'm sure the road will be well signposted. I just need to go downstairs first; I need to see my father.'

The lounge room was alive with candles as Marian stepped into the room. *Christine's getting desperate,* Marian thought, noting the romantic atmosphere.

'Dad, I need to talk to you. Could you excuse us please, Christine?'

From the look on Marian's face, Christine could see there was no room for argument. She tossed Therese's head and flounced out of the room.

'She's a very passionate woman,' Craig said. 'She reminds me more and more of your mother every day.'

'There's something I need to tell you – it's about Mum.'

'Oh, yes? What is it?' Craig said, realising with a stab of guilt that they didn't talk much about Sonia anymore.

'I've seen her.'

'You mean, like one of your spirits? I thought once they passed into paradise that was it.'

'I was able to get as far as the gate.'

'To paradise? What are you talking about?'

'Yes, what *are* you talking about?' Christine said. She'd only gone as far as the hallway so she could still hear what was being said.

'This is between my father and me.'

'We don't have any secrets, do we Craig?' Christine said.

'Therese left me. I know there are reasons for that but I can't accept them as excuses.'

Christine put a triumphant smile on Therese's face and sat down next to Craig. 'I'll never leave you,' she said, looking at him adoringly.

Marian held her breath as she waited for him to answer.

'You were sent here for a reason,' Craig said, looking back at Christine with obvious affection.

Well, that's it then, Marian thought. 'Why you were sent here, and by whom, doesn't seem to matter anymore,' Marian said. She left the room quietly and headed back upstairs.

'Is everything alright?' Jasper said as Marian strode out onto the balcony.

'I want to take my chances at that black gate,' Marian said. 'I want to face them down there. They won't hurt me – they want me.'

'It's much too dangerous, Marian.'

'Ha! That's rich coming from someone who was sent to trap me, to get me down there in the first place.'

'That was before I knew you, before I had these feelings for you.'

Marian let Jasper take her in his arms. She let him sweep her off her feet as they floated up in the air together. The whirlpool appeared beneath Marian's feet. She didn't let go of Jasper as she let it pull her down, down to the grey and dismal. As the pockets of fire came into view, Marian could feel her resolve strengthen. She remembered the last time she was here, how the horde of desperate souls reached for her and how she had abandoned them. *Not this time,* she thought.

* * *

Gregory's fire had shown him Marian's second coming. He wouldn't let her get away this time.

'I'm not hiding again,' Raven said, standing by Gregory's side. I'm ready to face her.'

Gregory barely heard her as he imagined his triumph when he delivered Marian into The Blackness.

'So, you came crawling back,' Marian said, when she and Jasper alighted in front of him. She ignored Raven altogether. 'I'm on my way to The Black Gate. Would you care to come along?'

Gregory tried to conceal his shock as he realised Marian's intentions. 'What is it you hope to achieve?' he said, struggling to retain his composure.

'I just want to talk to them.' Marian turned her back on the fire and peered out into the complete darkness and beyond. Fear turned to anger igniting the light Marian possessed. It shone from her body in a radiant stream, cutting through the darkness. As she ventured forward, inanimate souls came to life, attracted like moths to a flame, providing a silent escort. There was no grabbing or pushing as there had been before, just an orderly line behind her.

They know I mean to help them, Marian thought, as she turned to look at the growing flock. Then her eye caught on the one lone figure left behind.

'Come on then, Raven. It'll be no fun without you,' Marian said.

Gregory took up his position next to her, not content to be caught amongst the common rabble. A black gate came into view, all heavy bars and sadness. Marian slowed her progress, alert and ready for danger. All was silent as she approached her target. There was no sign of life, only a solid blackness that seemed to stretch beyond the gate to eternity. Her light lit up the darkness, revealing a desolate hopelessness that dispelled Marian's fear, replacing it with an agonising pity that tore her heart into a million pieces.

'I'm here. Show yourselves,' Marian said, reminding herself that evil languished behind these bars. She gave them a shake, the noise echoing far away.

'They won't come into the light. They rejected that eons ago,' Gregory said, shading his eyes from Marian's dazzling brilliance.

Marian let her anger go and, as it dispelled, her light dimmed and a soft glow replaced the bright white. There was a slight movement, then another, until seven black outlines stood behind the bars.

'Here she is, just as you commanded,' Gregory said.

'Silence!' the seven figures cried in unison. They came closer to the bars – closer to Marian. As they stared at her, features filled in their outlines. They were the same, but different – joined together, but separate.

'You show great courage appearing before us of your own free will,' one said.

'Yes, you're magnificent,' another said.

'I didn't come here to listen to empty words,' Marian said.

'Why did you come?' a third said.

'To see if these bars will open.'

'As you can see, there is no door, no lock. Souls are vaporised as they meet the bars. They then cease to be. But we are the caretakers of the gate. We exist to ensure no-one escapes their fate.'

'Then Therese is gone and you're trapped where you belong.'

'But we still exist and you can free us.'

Marian recognised the desperation in their voices. 'Where is she? I want to see her.'

'She no longer exists. She has become one with The Blackness.'

'But she didn't mean to take her own life. She was under an evil influence.'

'The crime was committed. The reasons do not matter. Forgiveness is not an option here.'

Marian backed away from the bars. She let her anger ignite the brightest of the light within her. Like a beacon, she scoured beyond the bars but there was nothing but emptiness. 'I have no more to say to you, except this. I will take any soul with me who deserves forgiveness. I shan't let you swell The Blackness with souls that ask for a second chance.' Marian turned towards her horde of followers. 'Who of you wishes to dwell in the light?'

'You can't take them. I won't allow it,' Gregory said, turning towards the traitors.

'You once embraced the light, Gregory,' Marian said. 'Wouldn't you like to feel its warmth again?'

Gregory stared at the bars, at his future and oblivion. Then he envisioned The Magenta Sky and he saw Imogen smiling at him the way she once did.

'All I ever wanted was to find my way back to her,' Gregory said.

'Are you willing to ask for forgiveness?' Marian said. 'Are any of you?' She held her breath as she watched the horde divide. Some souls reached for the black bars, immediately vaporising on contact, becoming nothing but wisps of the black smoke of non-existence.

'You promised me I would rule here,' Gregory said, turning back towards the bars.

'You are fit for nothing,' one of the seven said. 'You ran, cowering in the face of this girl. You lost the courage to face her.'

'Yet here we are, she and I on this side, with you seven trapped on the other,' Gregory said.

'Even if I had the power, I would release none of you. You will fulfil your destiny of guardians of The Black Gate, here to receive all those who shun forgiveness,' Marian said. She acknowledged at last that Therese had committed her crime long ago when she had refused to accept her gift. Now she was nothing and with the man she had followed into nothing. Marian began to back away from Hell.

'No, you must help me. I want to live again,' a seventh cried.

'You are dead. You're guilty of showing no compassion and none will be shown to you,' Marian said.

Seven pairs of black, gnarly hands grabbed the bars. They began to shake and screech like banshees as they realised all their plans had gone awry.

Marian moved closer towards the bars, letting her light shine its brightest. *Burn, baby, burn,* she thought.

'You would have taken all you could from Marian and then discarded her like she was nothing. Look at her … she's everything,' Gregory said. He had finally made his choice – to accept the light.

'Are you with me?' Marian said, hardly daring to believe Gregory was championing her.

'I want my dead life to mean something,' Gregory said, turning away from the black bars and the screams of Hell.

The End

About the Author

On any given day, Karen Element has a million story ideas rattling around her head. Turning her ideas into stories provides an outlet for her vivid imagination. When she is not writing, she loves travelling to far-off places, where she collects even more inspiration for her writing.

This is Karen's first novel. She lives in Brisbane, Australia with husband Michael.

www.ingramcontent.com/pod-product-compliance
Lightning Source LLC
Chambersburg PA
CBHW051426170626
46809CB00006B/2345